Dawson: The sea of love is not running smoothly for Dawson. But a night alone with Joey could be the night that makes it all right again.

Joey: Things seem just too good to be true with Dawson. What *do* their kisses mean, exactly? And is it her imagination or is Jen angling for him again?

Pacey: He's hooked on that sexy voice he hears, but its owner is not a 10 on the Pacey scale. Should he throw his fish back in the sea or will he miss out on the catch of a lifetime?

Jen: She volunteers to help find her friends who are floundering in the wilderness, but instead she stumbles across cute artist Steve.

DAWSON'S CREEK™

Dawson's Creek™

Calm Before the Storm

Based on the television series "Dawson's Creek™"
created by Kevin Williamson

Written by Jennifer Baker

POCKET BOOKS
New York London Toronto Sydney Tokyo Singapore

This book is a work of fiction. Names, characters, places and incidents are products of the author's imagination or are used fictitiously. Any resemblance to actual events or locales or persons living or dead is entirely coincidental.

An *Original* Publication of POCKET BOOKS

POCKET BOOKS, a division of Simon & Schuster Inc.
1230 Avenue of the Americas, New York, NY 10020

ISBN: 0-671-02475-2

First Pocket Books printing October 1998

10 9 8 7 6 5 4 3 2 1

Printed in the U.S.A.

Calm Before the Storm

Chapter 1

It was a perfect fall day. Glittering slate-green ocean in every direction, as far as the eye could see. A dramatic patchwork of silvery gray clouds and brilliant blue sky overhead. The bracing freshness of the salt air. The day crisp but not bitter cold. A few gulls trailing the modest but sturdy ferryboat. Joey leaned against the starboard railing and took a deep breath of clean sea air. *The Portuguese Princessa*—even the name of the boat was perfect. Storybook-like.

Or should have been. In someone else's movie.

Joey sighed to herself. Next to her, Dawson seemed to take her sigh for one of happiness. He smiled at her—a private smile. A slow, sexy, intimate smile.

Yup. Perfect. The young lovebirds with their not-so-secret secret. Fresh memories of their shared kisses. Their feelings for each other smoldering clandestinely, oblivious to the friends and classmates around them on the boat.

Except that it didn't seem to be working that way.

Joey cast Dawson a sidelong glance. Deep-set hazel eyes under thick sandy-colored brows, strong nose and mouth, commanding face. Sun-streaked blond hair. Handsome. A definite babe. And smart. Sensitive. Funny. Joey's friend, her best friend, and the guy she'd been dreaming about for . . . well, for a long, long time. Afraid to even admit she'd been dreaming about him because she'd wanted him so badly.

And finally he'd returned her feelings. The kisses they'd shared the other night still burned in her mind. The softness of his lips on hers—turning to eager intensity. His large palm stroking her hair. The way they'd drunk each other in, as if they couldn't possibly get close enough. As if they never, ever wanted to stop. Joey's cheeks got warm just thinking about it. It was incredible.

But in the bright, crisp, head-clearingly cool light of day, she wondered if being together was the right thing to do. What had those kisses meant? Were they for real? What would happen to their friendship now?

"What?" Dawson asked, studying her face.

Joey shook her head. "Nothing." She felt uncomfortable under his gaze. "I—um, I guess I had too much o.j. at breakfast. I'll be back in a sec."

"Yeah, sure, Joe," she heard Dawson say quizzically even as she beat a retreat from the deck of the boat.

She nearly bumped into Jen on the little staircase that joined the upper and lower decks. Jen was making her way up, a pair of binoculars in her hand.

" 'Scuse me," Joey said, squeezing by her.

"Joey. Are you all right?" Jen's voice was full of concern. "You're not getting seasick, are you?" she asked.

"Seasick? Last time I checked, it was as calm as a lake out there," Joey answered brusquely.

"Oh. Good. Well, hurry back," Jen said. "We're almost at Stellwagen Bank. You don't want to miss the whales."

"Whatever," Joey muttered, continuing down the stairs. Did Jen think if she was extra nice to Joey, Joey wouldn't notice the way she'd been oozing all over Dawson lately?

Joey entered the cramped, stuffy ferry bathroom. Jen had gotten her chance with Dawson already, and she had thrown it away. Why did she have to start laying on the New York charm again now that . . . Well, now that what?

Joey locked the door behind her, unzipped, and sat down on the thinking seat. Now that it was her turn? But was it really? She couldn't deny the reality of Dawson's kisses, or the sincerity in his hazel eyes. And he'd been super sweet all morning, showering her with smiles whenever no one else was looking.

So what was the deal with Joey's stomach? Why did she feel like she was hosting a wash and dry cycle internally? Why was Dawson making her feel so nervous all of a sudden?

Did her uncertainty have to do with Jen? Well, that certainly could be part of it. What if Dawson wasn't totally over her? What if Joey let herself believe—let herself really fall for the idea of Dawson and Joey, Joey and Dawson, only to have Dawson go back for another rewrite? Decide the hero should end up with the curvy blonde who'd breezed into town?

And then there was the timing factor. A couple more weeks and Joey could be learning about romance the French way. A semester in Paris. Far, far from Dawson and Capeside. *Au revoir, tout le monde.* Funny how Dawson had turned Romeo right about the time she'd applied for her passport. Right about the time he'd had to start thinking about Capeside without her. What if she decided to stay? Would Dawson suddenly start thinking of her as ole pal Joey again? As soon as the plane had lifted off without her and she was stuck in Capeside and he had her where he wanted her?

Just go for it, Joey told herself. Stop thinking about it so much. Dawson's fault. Somewhere along the way she'd caught his habit of analyzing everything to death. Carpe diem. Seize the day. Except something was holding Joey back.

Suddenly the boat rolled portside. Joey gripped the steel railings on the sides of the stall. Above her head, from up on deck, she could hear the faint but unmistakable collective gasps and excited squeals of her classmates. Whales! Joey finished up and raced out toward the action.

"Just ahead, at about one o'clock, you can see the fluke—that's part of the tail—of a male humpback whale," said a deep voice over the boat's loud-speaker system. It was Dr. McCann—"You can call me Jim"—from the Oceanographic Institute, a ruddy, round man with a bushy gray beard who was leading their field trip out of the Capeside harbor. "There seems to be another one just under the surface at about three o'clock," he added, using the points of a clock to illustrate the positions of the huge mammals.

Joey rushed up the narrow staircase. Jim McCann continued to track the whales' positions, like a radio announcer recounting a play-by-play of some big baseball game.

"One o'clock. There he goes! Right out of the water! Okay, diving down again. There's the tail—straight up. Means he's diving deep. Probably won't come up again right away."

Joey burst onto deck and scanned the ocean. "Oh!" their guide's voice exclaimed excitedly. "Starboard side! Ten o'clock! There's the female—and she's breaching! Look at her! Right out of the water!"

The boat rolled to the other side as everyone dashed to starboard. Joey saw the enormous creature split the surface of the water nose first and shoot straight up like a rocket. She heard her own shriek of delight meet dozens of others in the salt air. My God, the whale was absolutely huge! And beautiful! The whale arched over the water and sliced back into it smoothly. The water splashed up in fountains of white foam around her.

Joey caught sight of Jen jumping up and down excitedly, grabbing Dawson's arm, pulling him into an impetuous hug.

Suddenly Joey felt her own excitement snuffed out cold. Dawson was smiling just a little too broadly. Okay. So all their schoolmates and teachers were smiling, too. But still . . .

As if feeling her eyes on him, Dawson turned and spotted Joey. His smile only got bigger. He motioned her over with a big wave. "Joey! They're jumping right out of the water! Come on!" he hollered.

Jen took her hands off Dawson. Joey made her way over and squeezed in between him and Pacey. Dawson leaned over to her. "I missed you," he whispered in her ear.

Joey managed a small smile. Okay, so maybe she was making too much of Dawson and Jen. But there was still something inside her that was holding back. Something that wouldn't let her just melt into Dawson's arms. What was it about finally getting what you wanted? Thought you wanted. No, wait. She did want Dawson. Had always wanted him. Still wanted him. It was just . . . what? That she needed to make sure she wasn't going to get hurt?

Something like that. It sounded good, at least.

"There's the bull again. One o'clock," said Jim, his voice amplified across the deck.

Joey rushed with everyone else to the other side of the boat. She felt herself gasp as the whale surfaced—massive, sleekly gray-black with a giant steel-white belly. If Joey had been in the little rowboat she used to ferry herself to Dawson's house, that creature could have swallowed her and the rowboat in one bite, just about.

"And there's another one at two o'clock," Dr. McCann said. "Look at him slapping his flukes against the water. That's called lobtailing, and no one's really sure why they do that. A show of strength? A mating ritual? Or maybe it's just fun. Oops—there's the female again!"

Everyone was running from one side of the boat to the other and back again. Exclamations of delight and amazement rose in the salt air.

"A male and a female," Dr. McCann said. "Now, humpback whales are known to mate for life. Once they find each other, that's it."

"Yeah, that's what they *say,*" Pacey wisecracked.

Dawson looked at Joey, rolled his eyes, and laughed.

Joey managed to laugh, too. But she couldn't help thinking that those whales had it made. At least they knew exactly what—or who—they wanted.

Chapter 2

"It looks like there's a calf swimming next to the female," Jim McCann pointed out. "See the shadow right below her belly? Now, whales are mammals like us; they're not fish. They give birth to live young, which they nurse."

Pacey strained toward three o'clock for a better view. He and everyone else on the trip.

"Humpback whales give birth to a single calf," Jim noted. "Twins are extremely rare and usually don't survive."

"Well, if you had to give birth to a baby that size, you might not be up for more than one, either," a new voice quipped. A female voice. A low, throaty, sexy female voice.

Pacey was instantly more interested in the source of that voice than in the calf. He swiveled around and peered up into the wheelhouse. Big Jim

McCann sat at the ship's wheel, steering gently and spilling information into his microphone. There was someone sitting behind him, partially blocked from Pacey's view. Pacey had noticed another person in the wheelhouse earlier. Noticed in a vague way. One of Dr. McCann's assistants from the institute, he figured. He hadn't paid much attention to her. Until now.

"The cow shoots the milk through the water into the calf's mouth," Dr. McCann said. "It's a thick, rich substance with a high fat content, and the calves gain thousands of pounds in a few months."

"Milk. It does a body good," the girl put in.

Sexy voice and funny, too. A sharp wit. Pacey was captivated.

"My daughter, Sylvie," Jim told the whale watchers. "Home from prep school for a few days to spice up her old man's dry scientific lecture."

"You mean wet scientific lecture," Sylvie joked.

Everyone from Capeside had turned to get a glimpse of Sylvie. Pacey could see her cloud of red hair behind her father, but the rest of her remained just out of sight, from this angle. A saucy redhead. Well, well . . . that had some definite possibilities.

"There! By the stern! The bull has surfaced again!" Dr. McCann called out. "Breaching! Right there by the boat! Folks, not everyone gets to see this so close up."

Sylvie was forgotten. By everyone but Pacey. His classmates craned their necks toward the back of the boat, oohing and ahhing in harmonious delight. But Pacey kept his sights on the wheelhouse, shifting positions for a better view of Sylvie.

A mermaid. An exotic sea princess. A beach beauty extraordinaire. Daryl Hannah in *Splash.* Bo Derek in *10.* All those *Baywatch* girls—but with humor and brains as big as their . . . whatever. If only Pacey could get a magnified view inside the wheelhouse.

And then a flash of brilliance like rays of sunshine bursting out of the clouds and striking the water. "Jen," Pacey said, turning toward her. Jen stood slack-mouthed, ogling the breaching whale. "Jen, let me use your binoculars for a sec."

Jen held out the binoculars without taking her eyes off the whale. "Pacey, the creature's as big as an apartment building," she said. "What do you need these things for?"

Pacey took them and started easing his way out of the throng of Capeside students.

"Where are you going with them?" Jen asked, without turning. She made no move to follow him. "Oh, my God, Dawson, would you look at the size of his tail," he heard her say.

"I always knew you were a secret size queen," Pacey thought he heard Joey mutter.

He left his friends to do their three-is-a-crowd routine for the whales. Coming around the stern of the boat to the starboard side, he raised the binoculars toward the wheelhouse. In his mind's eye, he saw a flame-haired goddess with an incredible voice. Through the binoculars—a complete blur.

He adjusted the focus. The back of Dr. McCann's head swam into view. The goddess's father. Pacey made a slight alteration in his viewing direction, holding his breath in anticipation.

She was . . . completely disappointing. Pacey let his breath out noisily. Sure, Sylvie was probably perfectly nice. But she had her father's thick features and hefty girth. Not exactly ugly, but no mermaid, either. No Heather Locklear. Or any sexy, sylph-like Heather at all. Pacey let the hand holding the binoculars drop to his side.

Nope, he wasn't going to find any sea goddesses on this trip. Might as well go back and see how those whales were doing.

Dawson directed the scene in his mind. The young man and the young woman out at sea. A light wind in her soft, dark hair, the two young lovers with their faces toward the ocean. King of the world. With Joey his queen. The earnest but heretofore misguided hero looking for love in all the wrong places and finally finding it was right in front of his eyes all along. Strings, harps, cherry blossoms bursting into bloom. Okay, no cherry blossoms. They were out to sea, after all. But that was the least of it.

The major problem was that Joey wasn't following the script. She'd been distant and impossible to read all day. Joey—Dawson's closest friend, the girl whose thoughts he could finish, and who finished his thoughts just as easily. The one who always understood him, and vice versa.

And now Dawson had absolutely no clue what was going on in her head. What was it all about? Was she feeling shy with all their friends and classmates around? Since when had Joey ever been shy with Dawson? Then again, since when had Joey ever kissed Dawson the way she had recently?

Over on the other side of the boat, she was discussing something with Marla Adams and Dr. Rand, the science teacher who had arranged this trip. Imitating the arc of a breaching whale with her hand, Joey was more animated with them than she'd been with Dawson since they'd left Capeside. Did she hate the way he kissed, or what? Sure hadn't seemed like it before.

Dawson leaned heavily against the railing. Joey looked so pretty today. Even in a simple pair of jeans, a windbreaker zipped over her heavy turtleneck sweater. So pretty and so natural. And he wanted her so badly.

Of course, he'd wanted Jen just as badly, hadn't he? Dawson felt the corners of his mouth turn down in a frown. And what had come of that? When she'd finally spent the night in his bed, he was over her. He hadn't so much as offered her a chaste kiss. And that same day—the day he woke up with Jen in his bed—he'd wound up passionately kissing Joey. Who he thought was his friend. Period. As in, I like you, but not like *that*. Somehow everything had gotten turned upside down and inside out. Everything had changed.

What if Joey went off to France, and Dawson's heart flew off with her? He didn't even want to write that scene.

"Pondering the mysteries of the deep, my fine friend?" Pacey's voice broke into Dawson's confusion.

"Oh. Hey. Yeah, well, pondering some mysteries.

Of another species, in fact, not of the aquatic kind," Dawson replied.

"Aha," Pacey pronounced knowingly. "Doesn't take a marine scientist to know what lovely, totally mind-boggling species you're talking about, Dawson my boy. Who is it today? Betty or Veronica?"

Betty or who? "Excuse me?" Dawson asked.

"Dawson, Dawson." Pacey shook his head. "Didn't anyone tell you that there was more to childhood than watching one movie after another? Some of us had our noses buried in comic books, too. You know, Betty and Veronica from the Archies? They're classics. Some of the original editions are worth a bundle."

"Pacey, what are you talking about?" Dawson felt a flicker of irritation. Overhead a gull screeched.

"Betty—blonde girl next door. Veronica—dark-haired. Both in love with Archie. Archie, the good sport, friend to all, hero of the series. Kinda like you, Dawson. So which one do you want? And believe me, Dawson, I wish I had your kind of problems."

Dawson let out a long breath. "The problem is . . . well, it's always about timing, isn't it? Who wants who when. Who knows what who's thinking at any particular moment. Can we ever really know another person's thoughts?"

Pacey leaned against the railing next to Dawson. "You think too much. Maybe if I keep repeating that like a mantra, one day you'll get the point. You think that bull whale is out there thinking, 'The blond one or the brunette one?' By the time he decides, they'll both be down in the Caribbean with some more decisive he-whale."

Dawson turned to face his friend. "Is that why you're seeing so much action, Pacey? You be the he-whale, okay? You go get the girl."

Dawson could see he'd hit Pacey where it hurt. Pacey pouted. "There aren't exactly any mermaid types around here. Just the same old Capeside females we've been going to school with since before they got their first training bras. Oh, sorry. No disrespect meant to the ladies."

Dawson said mildly, "Sometimes the ones you've known forever turn out to be the mermaids."

Pacey's pout vanished. "Oh, I see, now. It's Veronica. Well, actually, Jen's more the Veronica type. Based on their personalities, I mean. But I was talking Veronica as in dark hair. As in a certain girl *you've* known forever."

"Yeah, okay. I was thinking about Joey," Dawson admitted. "Look at her. Definitely mermaid material."

"A mermaid who's swimming away across the ocean to France, perhaps?" Pacey commented.

"What am I going to do if she goes? I thought Joey and I had . . . well, I kind of thought we'd reached a new understanding," Dawson said, without going into detail. Even though he was playing certain particularly nice details over in his head. But he wasn't about to kiss and tell.

He didn't have to. Pacey might be a total goof-off. The class clown. But he wan't stupid. He arched an eyebrow. "Yeah?" he said, managing in that single syllable to convey approval and a little envy, without admitting that he actually knew anything. When it really counted, Pacey could be a true friend.

"Yeah, except since the second we left Capeside, she's been acting as if I was— I don't know. A fish or something," Dawson said. "And Jen . . . well, I would have done anything for her, for a while there."

"Yeah. I kind of remember something about that," Pacey deadpanned.

"And now that our ship has sailed, she's all of a sudden motoring back and making it clear she wants to try again."

"To put some new wind in your sails." Pacey was laughing at him.

"Okay, so maybe I'm taking the nautical metaphor a little—overboard." Dawson laughed, too. "But my pain is real."

"I feel your pain, bro," Pacey assured him. "But Dawson—you think too much. Love's not about thinking. It's about feeling." Pacey pounded his fist against his heart dramatically. "Whatever you do, do it. Don't just think about it. Don't just talk about it."

"The voice of experience," Dawson commented. "Thanks, Don Juan."

"Any time," Pacey replied. "Good luck, Dawson."

"Yeah. You, too. I hope you find your mermaid."

Chapter 3

"Next stop, Billings Island." Jim McCann's voice announced the itinerary.

Jen took a long breath of salt air. Most of her classmates had already gone down below after the boat had cleared Stellwagen Bank. Up on deck there was a chill in the air as the boat picked up speed. But Jen wanted a few more lungfuls of the salty breeze. She hadn't gotten over how nice it was to live by the ocean. Lifelong Capesiders barely noticed it anymore, except when hurricanes and high water took out the electricity and left a treacherous sheet of sand on the roads. But to Jen, it felt like a little bit of vacation every single day.

And the whales had been tremendous—in every sense of the word. It was one thing to see them in photos or on television. It was quite another to have a creature as huge as a New York City bus jumping out of the water so close to you, you could almost touch it.

"Billings Island," continued Dr. McCann, "is not really an island at all. It's a ten-mile strip of virgin barrier reef belonging to the National Seashore and connected to the Cape Cod mainland at one end."

"Well, actually, Dad, it's not a virgin," Dr. McCann's daughter put in. Jen felt her interest pick up. That girl, Sylvie, had a way of getting your attention. "Back in the old days there were some houses on it, and a tavern that the whalers used to go to—the whalers who plied their trade in the waters off Billings Island. And those whalers—well, they didn't have a reputation for traveling in the virgin crowd, if you catch my drift."

"Sylvie!" came Jim McCann's voice, muffled as if he had his hand over the microphone. "Excuse me, Dr. Rand," he added more clearly.

Jen laughed. The girl was definitely entertaining. With a smooth, low voice to beat that of any radio announcer.

"Dad, you're turning pink," Sylvie teased him. "Gosh, you can't say anything in front of these grown-ups. All I was really trying to point out was that Billings Island used to have houses and stuff on it. After the whalers moved on, Mom Nature reclaimed most of the land. And then in the sixties, when John F. Kennedy signed the National Seashore Act, the government got rid of the remaining couple of houses. So Billings Island got a second chance to be . . . pure unsullied land."

The way Sylvie rolled the word "pure" around on her tongue, stretching it out and making it sound even more R-rated than "virgin," got Jen laughing again. But the girl was smart, too. Knew her stuff.

"Thank you, Professor McCann," her father said. "So now you know. Billings Island is an eco-treasure of pristine pine forests and tidal flats. It's an unbeatable spot to observe some of our New England coastal vegetation and shore life. And it's . . . unsullied, as my daughter has shared with us."

Sylvie let out a rich laugh. "Right. I'll let you in on a little secret, though. There is one house that the Park Service seems to have missed. Or a piece of one. Out in the middle of the island, off all the trails and paths. It's pretty much impossible to find, unless you know about it. Of course, every high school kid on the lower Cape seems to know about it. The Love Shack, it's commonly referred to."

Jen laughed to herself and pulled her light jacket around herself more tightly. She took one more deep breath of ocean air and headed down to join her classmates.

Jim McCann's voice followed her through the loudspeakers. "But don't let my daughter give you any ideas, people," he said lightly. "Our agenda is a picnic lunch in a nice sunny little nook in the dunes I know about, followed by a nature walk. I hope you're all wearing sensible shoes."

Jen was greeted by Abby's wail. "Picnic? Walk? Oh, my God, I'm so sick I'm not gonna move from this bench." Abby was stretched out on one of the long plastic benches anchored to the cabin floor in rows. The back of her hand was draped on her forehead dramatically.

"Abby, you might feel better when you get off the boat," Marla Adams said levelly.

"Or maybe you won't," Pacey countered, from the bench behind Abby. "I mean, the sea's practically like a mirror out there. How can anyone get seasick on a day like this?"

"How long have you lived in Capeside?" Dawson got in on the act. "What, you say you've never been out on a boat, before?"

"Very funny," Abby moaned. "It may be calm now, but it's the calm before the storm."

"Right. Abby's so advanced she's got to be seasick before the rest of us," Dawson said.

Jen slid onto the bench next to Pacey, laughing a bit more than necessary at Dawson's joke. But it was Joey, not Dawson, who leaned past Pacey to shoot her a look. And it wasn't the friendliest look Joey had ever given her. Okay, fair enough. Maybe Joey was justified in feeling a bit irritated. But it wasn't as if Dawson had been responding in any serious way to Jen's extra efforts. They might be on a boat together, but she'd missed the boat with him. He'd made that clear enough when he left her in his bedroom that day to race after Joey.

But if Joey was thrilled to be playing Juliet to his Romeo, she wasn't showing it. What was up with those two, anyway? There had been some weird kind of tension between them all morning. It was about as obvious as the turbulent expression on Joey's face.

Jen didn't feel happy about this, either. Okay, maybe she wanted a second chance with Dawson Leery. Maybe she'd been a fool to let him get away.

But she liked Joey. And she knew Dawson liked Joey. And she could certainly try to get happy about the two of them being happy together. If they could get happy together, that was.

Jen sighed. Why did things always have to be so hard? If she'd thought life was going to be easier, less complicated in a small town, she'd been wrong. So maybe things didn't get quite as wild around Capeside. But she felt just as upended inside as she had in New York. You carried it all with you. It didn't change until you changed.

On the bench in front of them, Abby was a little more vocal than Jen in her misery. "Oooh, there is going to be a storm. It's coming. I know it."

"Tomorrow," Joey said, rolling her eyes. "The storm's supposed to hit tomorrow. Abby, you can't get seasick a whole day ahead of time."

"Actually, it looks like something's moving in pretty fast," Keith Silves, Marla's boyfriend, spoke up. He and Marla sat on the bench in front of Abby. He swiveled around to address Joey. "I know the folks from the institute are tracking that front, but I don't need any instruments to tell me it's moving in faster than they thought."

Jen felt a trill of nervousness. Keith was a fisherman, and Keith's father was a fisherman. He knew about those kinds of things.

Abby whimpered from her bench. "Oh, great! Stuck at sea in a storm. Tossed around like a leaf in this sardine can. Danger on the high seas—with you guys, no less."

Marla nudged Keith. "You're getting everyone freaked," she said. "Look, even if the storm hits early, it won't be till everyone's back home in Capeside. Right, Keith?"

Keith shrugged easily. "Right, Marla. I guess not."

"And the check is in the mail," Pacey had to add.

Jen felt a little wave of concern. But it was nothing compared to the tidal waves that could wash over a little boat in a storm. She knew that. She'd read that book, after all. The one everyone was reading on the beach a few summers back. The one about the swordfishing boat that went down—right about here, come to think of it. Off the coast of New England. "What if—what if we really do get stuck in a storm?" her voice came out sounding a bit too casual.

"Nah." Keith shook his head. "It's not rolling in that fast. Really."

"You'll be safe in Grams's house when it hits," Pacey assured her. "Right next door to Dawson. Very cozy. Betty. The girl next door." He addressed this last part more to Dawson than to Jen.

"Betty? Did I miss something?" Jen wondered out loud.

"Just that Pacey here is a jerk," Dawson said harshly.

"But will Veronica's Rolls-Royce be tied up to the dock, is the question," Pacey went on.

Oh. Tied up to the dock. As in Joey's little rowboat. As in Joey at Dawson's house. As in Betty and Veronica. Now Jen understood.

"Words stronger than 'jerk' come to mind," Joey said.

Jen let out a slow breath. Nope. Things weren't

any less confusing here than they'd been in New York.

Pacey listened to Sylvie's whiskey-smooth voice echoing through the cabin of the boat. He was just going to pretend that he hadn't seen what she looked like, that she could still turn out to be his busty mermaid. His funny, smart dead-ringer for the young Ursula Andress, emerging wet and lucious from the ocean in vintage James Bond. A boy could dream, couldn't he?

"Up ahead is the spot where the pirate ship *Whydah* sank in 1717," Sylvie was saying. "That's pure fact, guys. A real live pirate ship. Well, a real dead pirate ship, after 1717."

Pacey chuckled. He liked the girl. Liked his fantasy mermaid.

"It was loaded with loot, too," Sylvie said. "A few years ago they began a salvage and started bringing some of the ship and its cargo up from the ocean floor. But the best part of the *Whydah*, I think, is the story about its captain, the feared and notorious Sam Bellamy," Sylvie intoned dramatically.

"Ooh, a pirate story!" Jen exclaimed.

"Well, that lets us all out of talking to each other," Joey said, flashing a patently NutraSweet smile.

"Now, this one I can't guarantee as fact," Sylvie said. "But the story's been around for a long time."

Pacey leaned back and got ready for the show.

"Starts when Captain Sam—then just a young man who wasn't a captain yet—left his home in England for the New World. That's us, gang—the

United States, which wasn't the United States yet. No one's sure why Sam left the mother country, but he did," Sylvie added.

"Sick of hanging around the same old place?" Joey suggested.

"Had a chance to make his mark in the New World," Dawson proposed. "To be someone."

"Nah." Pacey shook his head. "It was some scandal, for sure. Ole Sam got into trouble back in England—got involved with the wrong girl, whatever—and the powers that be sent him away."

Joey laughed. "The wrong girl didn't happen to be an English teacher, did she?"

"Ouch," Pacey said honestly. It still hurt to think of Tamara.

"I'm with Pacey." Jen cast her vote. "Definitely some scandal that got him sent away. Believe me."

Pacey heard Dawson click his tongue. "Hey, you guys. Do you want to hear the story or not?"

"Joey, you started it," Pacey reminded her.

"Sorry. Let the girl finish her story."

Pacey was only too happy to. Sylvie's voice was pure honey as it poured out of the loudspeakers. "He set out for Cape Cod—the lower Cape, not far from where we are right now—to stay with his aunt. There he met a girl named Maria Hallett."

"Some guys never learn," Pacey commented. Joey shot him a silencing look.

"Some people say Maria was a witch. That she enchanted Sam. I say stop making excuses for your feelings, guys, and take some responsibility for them."

Hearty laughter from the female set aboard the

Princessa. Pacey had to stifle a chuckle of his own. She knew how to tell a story, his sexy-voiced mermaid.

"Whatever the deal, of course Sam and Maria fell in love," Sylvie said. "But her parents weren't all that keen on him."

Murmurs of empathy could be heard from a fairly sizable number of Capeside High students.

"Maria's parents thought Sam wasn't a solid enough prospect. But that didn't stop Sam and Maria."

"Never does," Pacey said.

"They only grew more passionate about each other. More convinced they had found their soul mate. And so they married each other in secret, under the cover of night, in an apple orchard right on Billings Island, in fact."

"Of course there is no apple orchard on Billings Island," her father put in pragmatically. "Not now, there isn't."

"Well, there was," Sylvie said forcefully. "At least in this story."

"Man, someone needs to tell Dr. McCann about the willing audience and their leap of faith," Dawson said. "*I* can see it. The moonlight slipping through the branches of the apple trees, spilling onto their faces as they recite their vows, the sound of waves gently lapping the shore nearby . . ."

"But being secretly married didn't really change much," Sylvie went on. "Sam and Maria had to keep sneaking around to see each other. Her parents still disapproved of him.

"Well, then he heard about this Spanish fleet that

had gone down off the coast of Florida in a hurricane. The ships had been loaded with gold. Some of the Cape men organized a salvage mission, and Sam saw his chance for great wealth and status and a marriage that would pass muster with the in-laws."

Pacey chuckled.

"Now, Sam had spent some time on an English merchant ship back home, so shipping out to sea was a natural for him," Sylvie went on. "Except getting treasure off the floor of the ocean isn't easy even today. And this was nearly three hundred years ago. The trip was a flop. And Sam was ashamed to come home empty-handed. When one of the other men invited him to join a pirate crew, he said okay. You know, we've got our insider trading scandals, and they had their pirates."

"Good one," Pacey said approvingly. "History class should be so entertaining."

"The pirate route was more successful for Sam," Sylvie continued. "In fact, he was so good at it that his fellow pirates mutinied their captain and let Sam take over."

"Ooh, this is good," Dawson said gleefully. "*Mutiny on the Bounty* meets *Romeo and Juliet*."

"So Sam was off capturing ships all over the world and raking in the riches. And Maria was back home, waiting. And waiting. And as if it wasn't hard enough to have her brand-new husband gone, shortly after he left, she'd discovered she was carrying his child."

"Right. Up the ante," said Dawson admiringly. "Give every character more to lose."

"Well, you can imagine what the Puritans who settled these parts thought of that. The town elders sent poor Maria to live at the top of those dunes you can see across the water on the starboard side."

Pacey immediately turned to squint out the row of cabin windows. In the distance, mountains of sand rolled down to meet the flat green-gray sea. Nice place to visit, but you wouldn't want to live there, Pacey thought. Sylvie had him hooked. He wanted to know what happened next.

"So while she waited for Sam to come home, she managed to eke out a living weaving cloth—or casting spells, if you believe that version," Sylvie recounted. "And every night she walked the dunes, looking out to the sea and hoping to spy the lanterns of Sam's ship bringing him back."

"How sad," Jen whispered. And on this point, Joey nodded in agreement.

"Well, I guess Sam finally remembered why he'd gone to sea in the first place. And he had enough riches to buy Maria's parents and the town twice over. So he decided to head home. But he couldn't resist one last hit."

"They never can," Pacey heard Joey mumble.

"The *Whydah* was one of the biggest, fastest ships of its day, and it was carrying nearly five tons of treasure! Gold, silver, jewels . . . It led Sam's ship on quite a chase, and put up a good fight. Swords, cannons, guns, the works. I'm not so big on fight scenes, so I'll fast-forward, here."

"What happens when you let a woman direct," Dawson cracked to Pacey. Jen and Joey managed to land simultaneous slugs to Dawson's arms from either side.

"But in the end, Sam and his men were the victors," Sylvie recounted. "They swapped ships with the *Whydah's* crew because the *Whydah* was a better craft than the one they'd been sailing, and they moved all their loot and weapons onto the new ship. Then they headed for home.

"They never got there. You know the ending already. The *Whydah* lies buried right out where we're sailing now. There was a terrible storm, and maybe the *Whydah* was just too loaded down to be stable. All that treasure."

"Ah, the moral of the story," Pacey said.

"But you have to imagine it from Maria's side," Sylvie said. "There she is, watching for Sam's ship. She has their tiny baby in her arms. And she sees it! Finally! After waiting day after day, night after night, month after month. All the hardships she has endured are already melting into the past. She's bursting with happiness. Her Sam is a notorious pirate, it's true. But she feels a little different about that than she once might have. After all, the prominent, respected people of her community had simply cast her out, turned their backs on her in her time of need. If that's upright, she doesn't want any part of it. And now Sam is returning to her. To her and their child. And they won't be alone. . . .

"But then came the thunder, the lightning, the water rising in gargantuan waves."

Pacey felt himself poised at the edge of his seat. You couldn't help wishing for the *Whydah* to come through. Even though you knew it wasn't going to.

"They were so close to shore, Maria must have been able to see the whole thing. That was part of the problem, in fact. That they were in such shallow water. They tried to fight their way back out to sea, against the torrential winds."

"Why?" Jen's voice was full of puzzlement. "Why would they want to get farther away?"

"Easier to ride out a storm in deeper water," Pacey explained. That was pretty elementary when you'd grown up by the ocean. "Waves break in shallow water. There are rocks and sandbars and all kinds of obstacles."

"But the *Whydah* was doomed," Sylvie pronounced the death knell. "She capsized and broke up. Maria Hallett must have heard the wild ringing of the ship's bell, maybe even heard the sailors' screams being carried on the winds. She watched as Sam's ship went down. He never came back to her."

There was a moment of stark silence in the cabin of the *Princessa*. You knew how the story was going to end, but it was a blow nevertheless. Pacey voted Sylvie Most Valuable Player of this field trip, so far.

"Legend has it," she concluded, "that Maria Hallett's ghost walks the dunes to this day, waiting for the love who never made it home."

"Wow!" Jen said in a soft voice. "Can you imagine finding someone you love enough to wait forever for?"

"Oh, right," Joey said less sentimentally. "Someone who'd declare his undying love and then leave you to wander the dunes alone for all of eternity."

"Joe, he did it for her. For Maria. Because he loved her," Dawson said. "He couldn't be with her the way things were, so he decided to change things."

Joey frowned. "To rewrite the script, you mean. Well, maybe he should have been satisfied with what he had to begin with. Only it wasn't enough. He had to go out and get more. And he changed. And then he couldn't get back to her."

Pacey arched an eyebrow and slid down in his seat. No way he was going to get in the middle of this. Instead, he let his mind wander to Sylvie's honey-smooth voice and sharp wit.

Chapter 4

Joey turned her face to the sky and basked in the sun like a cat. It was cozy and surprisingly warm where she nestled, in a shallow dip in the dunes. Especially when the sun emerged from the clouds and beat down on the picnickers. Joey shed her windbreaker and took a long sip from her water bottle. Around her, the others were breaking out the brown paper bags and unwrapping the lunches they'd brought from home.

Dawson had a submarine-shaped sandwich on a long loaf of crusty French bread, stuffed with all kinds of cold cuts and fresh vegetables. Joey couldn't see him laboring over that in his kitchen. It was definitely the handiwork of his mother for her cherished only son.

Pacey, on the other hand, had a cold slice of last night's pizza dinner, a soda, and one of those packaged containers of fluorescent green Jell-O. "Hey, kids, it glows in the dark," he said, inspecting its contents.

Joey's lunch was more along those lines—a tuna sandwich she'd prepared in about five seconds this morning, without the essential addition of mayo, since no one had bothered to buy any after the last jar had run out. Until Bessie and Bodie's baby had arrived, her lunches had always benefited from Bodie's extraordinary culinary skills, and her willingness to try out his new creations. But Bodie didn't have time for that these days.

Next to Joey, Jen was unpacking one plastic container after another. Joey watched curiously. "Spanish egg pie with onions and potatoes," Jen said, tapping one container on its lid. "Carrot slaw with toasted sesame dressing." She pointed to another. "Poached pears. And Grandma's famous ginger cookies."

Joey was even less interested in her sandwich than she'd been a moment ago.

"Her church group's new cookbook just came out," Jen explained, taking out a plastic fork. "The cookies are the recipe she contributed. I remember them from when I was little."

"Looks good," Joey said enviously.

"You can share it with me," Jen offered. "She packed enough for an overnight. Especially the cookies."

"Oh. Well, if you're sure," Joey said. "Thanks."

"You're welcome. Besides, you can afford to eat all those cookies."

Joey wrinkled her brow. As if Jen was some double for a beach ball or something. Didn't she know that most of the girls on this trip would trade bodies with her in a second? Faces, too. But there was Jen, complimenting Joey. And sharing her picnic with her. Why did Jen have to be so nice to her?

The truth was, Joey had gotten to actually kind of like Jen. Or would have liked her if it weren't for the whole Dawson thing. Joey took a taste of the egg pie. She definitely liked Jen's grandmother's cooking.

Joey sneaked a look at Dawson. He was watching her. He flashed her a tentative smile. Her face grew warm, and she looked away. Dawson. Jen. Joey. Triangle. A geometrical figure having three angles and three sides. Any three-sided or three-cornered object. A situation involving three persons.

It had been simpler with Jeremy, her sax-playing surfer boy, who'd blown into her life and blown out. Fun, too. Or with Anderson Crawford, the babe-alicious prep school boy whose parents' yacht had been anchored at Capeside earlier this year.

But they weren't the ones she'd shared her dreams with. Not to mention all those nights watching every movie that had ever been made. They hadn't seen her through her mother's death. Or her father's arrest. They couldn't finish her sentences before even she knew what she was going to say.

Then why were Dawson's secret smiles and tender looks making her so nervous?

Joey tried to push the whole complicated deal out of her mind for a little while. To enjoy the moment. Here she was, snuggled in a valley of sand, with the sound of the waves just over the dune, the tall dune grasses rippling in graceful patterns as the wind picked up, the air clean and fresh, the sound of seagulls high overhead, and the happy voices and laughter of her classmates. And Jen's lunch.

Jen, not Dawson, seemed to read her mind this time. "It's so beautiful here, isn't it?" Jen said with a sigh. "You guys are so lucky to have grown up so close to all this unspoiled beauty."

"You mean you missed *Beach Blanket Bingo* growing up in New York?" Joey asked, without any edge.

Dawson jumped in. *"The Endless Summer?* Or how about *Suddenly, Last Summer?"*

"The Summer of '42," Pacey said, getting in on the game. He *would* come up with that one, Joey thought.

"Okay, okay," Jen laughed. "You win the name-the-summer-movie contest, Dawson. And your prize is . . . a job at Capeside's own Screenplay Video."

Joey laughed too.

"And besides, I *did* get to experience a little *Beach Blanket Bingo* in New York. I mean, I spent the summers out in the Hamptons. It's not as unspoiled as this, but it's pretty, and there are great beaches."

"The Hamptons?" Abby seemed to materialize out of nowhere. Last Joey had looked, she'd been lying on the sand nearby, recovering from her bout of seasickness. "The Hamptons, as in Uma Thurman and Ethan Hawke? Veronica Webb? Martha Stewart?"

"I never managed to spot any of them," Jen said easily. "I saw Christie Brinkley at a farm stand once. She picked up an ear of corn that I'd already inspected and put back. That's my one brush with Hamptons royalty."

"But the parties," Abby insisted. "I've read about all the glitzy, wild parties they have out there in their *Architectural Digest* homes."

Jen shrugged. "Well, if you read it . . ."

Joey laughed. Jen wasn't so bad, really.

"Come on, Jennifer," Abby prodded. "You did some of that Hamptons partying. Admit it."

There was a beat of silence. You could hear a particularly strong wave crash against the sand.

"Yeah, she partied," Dawson muttered. "She got wild."

Joey could hear his bitterness. And the thought he'd left unfinished. *She partied. She got wild . . . with everyone but me.* Joey's easy mood dissolved instantly. If Dawson was still so bent out of shape about that, it must mean it still really mattered to him. That Jen still really mattered to him. Way too much.

"Okay, guilty as charged," Jen said defensively. "So I went to some parties, Dawson. I even had fun. Is that such a criminal act? Wouldn't you have gone to a good party if you'd been invited?"

"*I* certainly would," Abby said. "It's just that we don't do parties in Capeside the way they do them in the Hamptons."

Suddenly, Joey felt a touch defensive herself. Abby was always implying that she was too sophisticated for Capeside, that she knew she belonged someplace bigger and better, that the rest of them were just a bunch of beachcombers. "Maybe you just weren't invited to the good Capeside parties, Abby. And besides, how do you know how they do parties in the Hamptons?"

Joey did, in fact, remember more than one beach party in Capeside that had gotten out of hand. There was one that had been enough to make her swear off even a drop of liquor for the rest of her life. She'd been pretty pathetic that evening. And Dawson? He'd been running after Jen all night. Trying to wrest her from the clutches of the old boyfriend who'd driven up from New York.

Joey frowned deeply. What if Dawson had caught Jen the way he wanted to—and kept her? He and Joey probably never would have wound up together.

The sun slid behind a dark cloud cover that stretched as far as the eye could see.

Pacey kept hearing that voice of his dreams behind him. He could barely pay any attention to what Dawson and the others were saying. Instead he let the low rhythms of Sylvie's words take him into a little daydream.

It was just the two of them here on Billings Island. They'd arrived in a little sailboat, working the sails and rudder in elegant tandem. They'd feasted on cold lobster salad and champagne, spread out on a linen picnic blanket. They'd made witty conversation. They'd laughed. They'd looked into each others' eyes. And of course she was the most beautiful woman he had ever laid eyes on.

Except she wasn't. Pacey kept telling himself not to turn around, but that was like being told not to think of pink elephants, and suddenly you couldn't get pink elephants out of your mind. He just couldn't refrain from taking a look behind him at the voice. Couldn't resist turning toward the low, sweet tones. And each time he did, he saw a perfectly normal, perfectly plain, slightly overweight girl, eating a sandwich and talking to her father and Dr. Rand.

And he'd turn back, disillusioned, and take a few more bites of his slice of pizza.

And then he'd hear her throaty laughter and darned if he couldn't help taking another look—just like he was doing now. And there she was. Same as she'd been the last time. Wavy red hair framing a round pink face with thick features and bright hazel eyes. Pudgy body in jeans and red warm-up jacket. Pacey's bikini dreams evaporated in a glance.

But before he had a chance to turn his back on her again, Sylvie caught his eye and smiled at him. A nice open, friendly smile. Pacey felt a flash of embarrassment, as if she had been able to read what he was thinking. He managed a stiff smile back. Okay. She wasn't his mermaid. No reason to be rude about it.

He didn't look Sylvie's way again.

As the clouds thickened and the wind blew stronger, everyone finished up the meal and began to clean up. Pacey stuffed his paper plate, plastic cup, and empty soda can into the brown lunch bag, and stuffed that into his knapsack to dispose of when they got back to civilization.

"Hello." Suddenly that voice was right there next to him.

Pacey whirled around and found himself face-to-face with her. With his non-mermaid. With Sylvie.

"Oh. Um, hi."

"I'm Sylvie."

"Pacey." He nodded awkwardly.

"I noticed you looking through your binoculars back on the boat," she said. "Did you see anything interesting?"

Pacey hoped his face wasn't turning red. Did she realize he'd been using those binoculars to check her out? He joked his way out of the question. "You mean like eighteenth-century ghosts walking around on the dunes?" He shook his head. "That was a great story," he added. "You ever get low on funds at boarding school you could consider pitching it as a sequel to *Titanic*. Prequel, actually. Way pre," he went on. He knew he was babbling, but after daydreaming about a fantasy Sylvie all morning, he felt weird talking to the real one. He just couldn't put the two Sylvies together. He focused on an imaginary spot somewhere behind her so that he wouldn't have to.

"Actually, I know someone who's writing a novel based on the *Whydah* story," Sylvie said. "She's from New York, but she summers around here."

"Cool," Pacey said, continuing to look past her.

"Yeah, I think so." Sylvie stood there. Pacey felt he was supposed to say something.

"So . . . that means you're from around here?" he asked.

"Well, I used to be," Sylvie said. "My folks moved to a small town about sixty miles from the Cape a couple of years ago, and I started school in another district. I have a few days off, for good behavior. They let me out on furlough," she said in her thick, rich voice.

Pacey laughed. "That bad?"

"Nah. Not really. I don't mind it. Well, they can get a little strict sometimes, but I miss it around here. I like to visit when I get the chance. Of course, when I lived here, it felt like there were about twelve people in the town and I knew them all and I knew everything about them and vice versa, and I couldn't wait to leave."

"Dune grass is always greener, you mean?"

Sylvie laughed. "Exactly." They stood wordlessly for a moment. Pacey kept looking at the imaginary spot. The wind whistled through the very dune grass itself. Then Sylvie turned and looked where Pacey was looking. "Um, am I missing something really fascinating?" she asked, as she turned back toward him.

"Huh?"

"What are you checking out back there that's so interesting?" Sylvie asked curiously.

A wave of embarrassment washed over Pacey. Embarrassment and shame. "Oh . . . nothing. Really. Um, I was—looking at those dark clouds gathering over that hill over there."

Sylvie glanced at the sky. "Yeah. Hope we don't have to cut the trip short because of the weather.

Well, we should get everyone moving, I guess. We might not have as much time as we thought."

"Right. Okay," Pacey said. He made sure to look right at Sylvie as he responded. So she wasn't Heather material. Ignoring the reality of the situation wasn't going to change it. Besides, he liked her. She didn't have to be a 10 to be his friend.

Chapter 5

"Maybe they should have warned us to train for this little walk," Dawson said to Joey.

"Yeah, well . . . I was kind of thinking we could use it as gym credit for the rest of high school," Joey answered. It was the first thing she'd said to him in several miles. Felt like several dozen. Through deep sand and hilly pine forests. With the football team and the cheerleaders out in front, leading the marathon aerobic jaunt.

Dawson now knew the names of plants and trees he'd seen a million times and never stopped to look at closely. And he'd gotten a ringside seat for a show of rich life in a tidal pool: shells, seaweed, crabs waving their claws around. It was interesting enough. Better than another day in the hallowed halls of Capeside High, but right this second Dawson wouldn't have minded taking the next hydroplane back to the boat, to rest his tired legs.

"Daddy, are we there yet?" Pacey wise-cracked to Dr. McCann's daughter. They seemed to be getting along famously—talking, laughing, and clearly enjoying the hike.

Which was more than Dawson was managing to do. It had been a real mistake to let that comment fly about Jen and her partying. It had just sort of slipped out, and Dawson had tried to apologize afterward, but Jen had definitely cooled off, along with the weather. At least toward Dawson. Now she was up ahead with Mr. Capeside High, the football hero of the school, Cliff Elliot.

And Joey . . . Dawson replayed the feel of their lips meeting, the perfume of her skin, the way his heart had been beating overtime. Now he felt his face grow warm, despite the growing chill in the air. It had been agony waiting for her to show up at school for the trip this morning. But she'd been about as friendly and open as a wall most of the day.

Joey. Jen. There had been that slender window of promise when he'd had both possibilities. Two paths to go down and the choice had been his. Now the only path was this long, never-ending nature walk.

The narrow dirt path opened onto a clearing in the pine trees and brush. Up ahead, Dr. McCann stopped. The rest of the group gathered around him. On the ground in the middle of the clearing Dawson could see a dark gray slate rectangle about the size of a coffee table. Shells and smooth colored stones and pieces of driftwood had been placed on top of it like offerings at a geologist's buffet.

"This is the tomb of a Wampanoag woman," Dr. McCann said. "The Wampanoags were the Native American tribe local to Cape Cod and the surrounding areas. Were and are. There's still a small Wampanoag population left, especially on the upper Cape."

Jen moved toward the tomb and touched one of the stones lightly. "Who was she?" she asked Dr. McCann.

Sylvie answered for her father. "No one knows. She may have lived around the time of Captain Sam and Maria Hallett. This is what's left of an old Native American burial ground. The National Seashore rangers had the stone added to remind visitors that this land was settled before the Pilgrims ever got here. People have left the stones and things as a kind of memorial."

The Capesiders stood in appropriate silence for a moment. Sylvie didn't have to add that the Wampanoag civilization had paid the price for the colonists' settling. The shells and stones and wood spoke as eloquently as any history lesson.

Dawson felt Joey give a little shudder next to him. It could have been the sentiment of the moment. It could have been the cold wind. He could have put an arm around her and warmed her up, but he didn't.

He thought they'd finally sorted out their complex feelings. But now he was just as confused as ever. If not more confused.

A fat, cold raindrop struck his face like a tear. And then another.

"It might be kind of a good idea to get back to the boat as fast as we can," Keith Silves said to no one in particular. He was casting his seasoned glance on the angry sky.

"How far away are we, anyway?" Dawson asked.

"Five miles," Sylvie said. "Maybe six."

A loud collective moan went up from the crowd of students. "Gee, where did I put my cell phone," Pacey said dryly. "If I could find it, I'd call us a cab."

They left the Wampanoag woman to her quickly dampening resting place and started hiking back toward the boat as quickly as their tired legs could go.

"Rain, rain, go away?" Pacey suggested.

Sylvie shook her head. "I don't think so, Pacey. It's gonna take more than the power of suggestion to head this one off." The rain was starting to fall fast and heavy. "By the time we get back to the *Princessa*, we're going to be wishing we'd packed a change of clothes."

"Or an umbrella," Pacey said. His jeans were already sticking to his legs. His hair was wet. His classmates grumbled as they tromped back along the now muddy trail. But Pacey wasn't minding it half as much as he might have. Sylvie was turning out to be excellent company. Even if she didn't look like Heather.

"You know, I read somewhere that umbrellas basically disappeared during medieval times, and they weren't rediscovered until the eighteenth century. I mean, talk about forgetting your umbrella!" Sylvie cracked.

Pacey laughed. "I bet you'd be great on one of those game shows. Umbrellas for two thousand, please. Legends of the sea pirates for five."

Sylvie grinned. "I *am* the trivia champ of my dorm at boarding school."

"Well, you make it a lot more bearable for a guy to be stuck marching around in the rain," Pacey commented.

"Thank you," Sylvie said, her deep, sexy voice tinged with happy embarrassment.

"You're welcome," Pacey said. They walked along in silence for a few moments.

He found himself slipping back into his little fantasy. The one with him and Sylvie alone on Billings Island. The one that had started with the lobster salad and the linen picnic blanket. The one in which Sylvie looked like a movie star. The one where he was now kissing her in the pouring rain. . . .

He sneaked a look at her, and the fantasy was immediately washed away. He felt a stab of regret go through him. Sylvie was probably way more interesting than any Heather. She could beat any one of those *Baywatch* babes in a game of trivia in two seconds flat. She was definitely funnier. And probably any one of the luscious maidens who populated Pacey's dreamworld would switch voices with Sylvie in a flash.

But she wasn't who he wanted her to be.

* * *

The sky had opened up. Rain pelted down sharp and cold, like liquid shards of glass. "I think I left my windbreaker back where we had lunch," Joey muttered to Dawson, as they trailed behind most of the others. She shivered in her wet, soggy sweater.

"Bad timing," Dawson said, "but we have to pass by there before we get to the boat. I'm sure we'll find it."

"I could kind of use it now," Joey said miserably.

Dawson gave her a long, studied look. Joey pretended not to feel his eyes on her. "Well . . . look, you can wear my jacket if you want," he offered.

"All you've got on under there is a T-shirt," Joey said.

Dawson didn't answer right away. "Oh, you noticed?" he finally ventured, after a moment.

"Huh? Noticed what?"

"You actually looked at me today. Noticed what I'm wearing," Dawson said.

Joey wrapped her arms around herself. "What is that supposed to mean, Dawson? You were wearing a T-shirt on the bus. You put your blue jacket on over it when we got on the boat—that one your mom got you for Christmas last year. So what? What's your point?" It was too wet and cold to play one of their games of verbal Ping-Pong.

"My point?" Dawson blew out a long breath. "Look, Joey, you're cold and I'm offering you my jacket. Do you want it or not?"

"I'd just get the inside wet if I put it on over my sweater," she said.

"Fine," Dawson said flatly.

"Dawson, you shouldn't be mad because I don't

want you to freeze in just your T-shirt," Joey said touchily.

"Joey, I think you know it's not about that," Dawson shot back. He stopped walking.

Joey felt a shudder of apprehension. She wanted to keep going, but she couldn't exactly leave Dawson standing there, staring after her. She paused.

"Joey . . . listen," Dawson began grimly.

Joey suddenly realized her bladder was absolutely, totally full to the point of bursting. "Dawson, hold that thought, okay? All that water I drank at the picnic—it's catching up with me. Or maybe it's this rain. You know that old trick of dipping someone's hand in water when they're sleeping. . . . Anyhow, why don't you go on ahead. I'm going to take a detour for a sec. I'll catch up with you guys."

"Again?"

Joey clicked her tongue in annoyance. "Yes, again." She stepped off the muddy path and waded into the brush and trees. When Dawson was out of her view, she squatted and did what she had to do.

She didn't hurry back to the path. The truth was, she knew she was being a little unfair to Dawson. She knew that sooner or later they were going to have to deal with what was happening between them. But she'd barely had time to get her mind around it, to believe it wasn't a dream, like she'd dreamed so many times before—or daydreamed, at least. And she still didn't know what it meant.

What if Dawson told her he'd made a mistake? A bells-clanging, fireworks-bursting, cymbals-banging, overwhelming kind of mistake. What if he told her he still liked Jen?

Or what if he told her he was wildly, madly in love with her? After half a lifetime of being "the friend," Joey just didn't know how she'd react to that one.

She stood in the forest, rain dripping off the ends of her hair. It was never, ever simple. You could want something and not have it. Or have it and be afraid to lose it. Or . . . well, she could probably stand here coming up with possibilities until the sun came out again.

Reluctantly she traced her way back to the path. Dawson was still standing there in his blue jacket.

"I thought maybe Captain Sam's ghost had carried you off," Dawson said.

"You didn't have to wait."

"I know," Dawson said.

"It isn't as simple for us as for you. We have certain logistical problems you don't have, going in the woods."

"I know," Dawson repeated.

"I guess we should try and catch up with everyone else," Joey said.

"I guess," echoed Dawson.

He seemed to consider saying something else, but then he turned and hurried up the trail.

Joey felt a pinch of relief. She jogged a little to keep up with him. He stepped up the pace until he came to a fork in the path atop a small rise. Joey stopped next to him.

Even in the driving rain, it was a spectacular vista. In one direction, undulating dunes and a sandy sweep of open space bordering a grassy marsh with rain-buffeted estuaries running through it. In the other direction, soft, thick pine groves and rolling hills. Nothing but nature as far as the eye could see. They were totally alone. Together. In a beautiful place.

Dawson looked into her eyes. They were standing so close to each other. Their faces were only inches away. "Joey?"

She could feel his warm breath on her damp face. Suddenly all the questions, the doubts, faded into a silent, alert awareness of their nearness. "Yes?" she whispered.

"Which way do we go?"

"Oh." Joey pulled back. She surveyed the view, again. Alone. No people. No classmates. No Dr. Rand. No Dr. McCann. She looked down at the muddy path. "The rain must have washed away everyone's footprints." She felt a trill of fear. "Dawson, I don't recognize any of this. Are we going in the right direction?"

Dawson shook his head grimly. "Which right direction? This direction or that one?"

Chapter 6

"Eureka!" Pacey said, as their group emerged from the patch of trees and the picnic spot came into view. Their boat was anchored just beyond those dunes. "The promised land!"

The mood shifted palpably among the wet, cold, tired hikers. Suddenly they seemed to get a second wind, and they nearly sprinted along the last stretch of the muddy path.

"Hey, Dad? We still have that hot chocolate mix on board?' Sylvie asked her father, as the group scrambled up the dune in the driving rain.

"You know, I think we just might," Dr. McCann confirmed.

"Good," said Pacey. "We could use a vatful. Maybe get right in there and take a hot bath." He reached the top of the dune.

And suddenly his good mood suffered a wipeout.

The ocean, calm and glassy when they'd left the boat, was looking a little like something out of *The Poseidon Adventure.* Waves were rolling in high and fast, beating the deck of the *Princessa* and causing her to rock like a toy. The water was white with angry foam.

Abby let out an oversize groan. "Please don't tell me we're getting back on that thing."

"We're not," Sylvie answered grimly. "Look at the launch."

Pacey followed her gaze to the motorized dinghy that had ferried them, small group by small group, from the the anchored boat to the shore of Billings Island. The dinghy had ripped free of its moorings and was out on the water, getting thrashed about mercilessly.

Dr. McCann and other adults from the boat rushed down toward the water for a closer look. Sylvie followed them. Pacey listened to the grim comments of his classmates.

"We must be what—ten miles from a road?" Marla Adams moaned.

Keith Silves put a protective arm around her, but he couldn't shield her from the worsening storm. A bolt of lightning split the gray sky, followed by a clap of thunder. "And the radio out there on the boat's not going to do us any good where we are," Keith said.

"It would have been nice of them to tell us we were going on an Outward Bound trip," Pacey said. He could feel the rain seeping right through his jacket.

Jen's voice rang out behind him. "Pacey, have you seen Dawson and Joey?"

Pacey turned around. Jen looked worried. He scanned the group gathered on the dune, then looked down toward the beach—just Dr. McCann and Sylvie and the institute people, shaking their heads and looking anxious. Pacey didn't spot anyone out on the trail, either—at least not on the part you could see from here. He looked back at Jen.

"They weren't with you?" Another streak of lightning lit up the sky.

Jen shook her head as the thunder boomed across the rough water. "I was talking to Cliff." His majesty the esteemed quarterback himself was standing next to Jen, his letter jacket soggy.

"They weren't with you?" Jen echoed Pacey's question.

"Uh-uh," Pacey said. He'd spent most of the hike with Sylvie.

"What are we going to do?" Jen asked, alarmed.

"That's a good question for all of us," Cliff said grimly.

"What if something happened to them?" Jen reached out and tugged on Pacey's wet sleeve.

Pacey felt a ripple of nerves. He'd last seen Dawson and Joey a few miles back, straggling behind everyone else. "Give them a few minutes. They'll catch up," he said uncertainly.

"Sure they will," Cliff said, more firmly.

"Maybe . . . maybe they wanted a little privacy," Pacey added, trying to convince himself as much as anyone else. "You know, a chance to get to know each other better, right?" He made a lame attempt at humor.

"Hey, looks like a certain marine biologist's daughter wanted to get to know *you* better, there, Witter," Cliff commented with a meaningful grin.

Pacey felt a bolt of embarrassment. "Yeah, well . . ."

"And there's a lot of her to get to know," Abby put in unkindly. "If you know what I mean."

Pacey knew. So did everyone within earshot. And now they were all looking at Pacey. If there had been a rock in the vicinity, Pacey would have hidden under it.

Cliff swallowed a laugh. Jen shot him a stern look.

Pacey felt his face getting hot. "Listen, I came to watch whales, not to get to know them," he cracked.

Jen sucked in her breath. "Pacey!" she said harshly. But she was looking behind him, not at him.

Pacey whirled around. He felt every muscle in his body tense up. There she was. Sylvie. Coming up right in back of him, her round face crinkled up in unhappiness. She had heard every word he said, and she knew who he was talking about. There was no question about it.

"Sylvie," Pacey croaked.

She let out a choked sound and raced back down the dune. Pacey took a few steps after her. Then he stopped. He looked back at Jen and the rest of them. They were all staring at him.

Pacey wouldn't have minded if one of those lightning bolts had struck him right then and there. Sylvie hated him. He'd made her feel horrible, and he hadn't even meant what he said. Everyone on the trip knew he was a major loser, Dawson and Joey were AWOL, and they were all at the mercy of a violent storm, right smack in the middle of absolutely nowhere.

Pacey took a deep breath and jogged down the dune after Sylvie. But he didn't hold out much hope for getting himself out of this one. Luck didn't seem to have come along on this field trip.

Dawson and Joey were going around in circles. At least Dawson thought they were. "Didn't we already pass that tree? The one that looks like a tall, scrawny skeleton?" he asked.

Joey frowned. "Dawson, this isn't one of your horror movies."

"No, it isn't," Dawson agreed. "It's a real live horror story, Joey. Me and you lost on a sandbar in the middle of the ocean, in a storm." He didn't add the part where there was so much unspoken tension between the heroine and the hero that you could cut it with a camping knife. Except they didn't have a camping knife. Or a compass. Or anything else that two people out in the woods might need.

"I told you that you should go on ahead, Dawson. I told you not to wait for me back there," Joey said.

Frustration ripped through Dawson like another lightning bolt. "You're saying you would rather be going around in circles by yourself?"

Joey was silent for a moment. "It's not a question of that," she said.

"Then it's a question of . . ." Dawson's unfinished sentence hung on the rain and fog.

They slogged forward half blindly along the soft, wet trail. "It's a question of maybe you'd rather be lost with someone else," Joey finally said.

Dawson stopped walking. It didn't seem to matter whether they went backward or forward anyway. "Someone else. Joe, doesn't what's between us mean anything?" he said softly. He didn't know whether to be hurt or angry or just absolutely, totally baffled.

"Look, Dawson, I saw how it made you feel when Jen was talking about the Hampshires."

Jen. Was this all about Jen? Still about Jen? Dawson blew out a long breath. "The Hamptons, Joey. Beach paradise to the rich and famous. Spielberg's been spotted there with his family."

"Hey, I wonder if Jen got wild with *him*," Joey said flatly. "Get over it, Dawson. She's played hide-the-salami a few times. You haven't."

Angry. He was definitely angry. Dawson felt his jaw grow tight. "You're right. I should have left you alone."

"See? That's what I was saying, Dawson. You don't want to be here with me. If you hadn't waited, you wouldn't be."

Dawson threw his hands up in the air. "Fine, Joey. Have it the way you want it. I wish I had gone ahead with everyone else."

"Especially a certain blond everyone else."

Dawson's anger was spreading like a puddle in the storm. "I could tell you that wasn't true, but what's the point when you refuse to believe me?"

"Dawson, can you honestly say that you wouldn't rather be inside the nice warm cabin of the boat with Jen laughing at your jokes and giving you her bright white smile?"

"Well, when you put it that way . . ."

"I knew it."

Dawson lost his last tiny drop of patience. "One thing I can say about Jen is that she acts as if she likes me, Joey."

"And you like her."

"Yes. I like her. I like Jen. She's my friend."

"Ah, the friend. Where have I stumbled across that before? The friend," she said scornfully.

Dawson's jaw clenched.

"Fine. What do you say we just pretend there's nothing between us." Neither of them said another word for a long, long time. They followed the muddy path to nowhere.

Joey glared at Dawson. Finally Dawson let out a tired breath. "Well, what do you want me to say, Joey? That I'm having a great time walking around lost and soaked and freezing and hoping the boat didn't leave without us?" he asked.

Joey paused and looked at him. He didn't know if the droplets on her cheeks were tears or rain. "Oh, God, Dawson. You think they did?"

"I don't know, Joey. Maybe if we can ever get back to where we dropped anchor, we'll find out."

Jen was as scared as she was wet. She pulled her almost useless sweater around her more tightly, but it just made her feel soggier.

"We should wait it out," Dr. Rand was saying.

"Stay here as a group. I don't want any more lost students on our hands."

A peal of lightning and thunder punctuated his words.

"How about french-fried students?" Abby said ominously.

"We're low enough down so the lightning's not going to strike us," Dr. Rand said. "It generally jumps to the water and the trees and the highest points."

Jen was glad to hear that. She guessed. Although it was hard to be glad about anything when you were this wet and miserable. And she was getting more and more worried about Dawson and Joey.

"I don't know if that's the wisest plan," Dr. McCann said. "We don't know how much longer it's going to take for this storm to let up. And once it gets dark, the temperature could take a drop. Between that and the wind, hypothermia is a real consideration."

Jen gulped. Hypothermia—as in so cold and wet that your body just sort of froze to death. Gee, she was so glad she'd moved away from big, bad, dangerous New York City.

"Someone's going to have to go for help," Dr. McCann concluded.

"And end up lost like my other two students?" Dr. Rand shook his head hard. "No. If anyone goes, we all go."

A chorus of protests split the stormy afternoon. "Another ten miles? I can't go another step."

"In this storm? Forget it. I don't want to be under any trees when they come down."

"All the way back where that Indian woman is? Farther? I'd rather take my chances swimming to the boat."

Jen understood exactly what everyone was saying. Who could walk another step? Still, she didn't feel very optimistic standing around here watching the boat get tossed and tumbled.

"Let me go," Sylvie spoke up. "I've been exploring the trails out here all my life. I'm not about to get lost. And I don't see much point in sticking around here," she said, with a pained glance at Pacey.

Jen felt a rush of sympathy for Sylvie. And maybe a little bit for Pacey, too. His remark had been cruel. No denying that. But she'd watched Pacey follow Sylvie down the beach, obviously apologizing profusely as they went. At one point he'd even gone down on one knee in an exaggerated, imploring gesture, trying to win her over with his particular brand of clowning.

But Sylvie wasn't buying. And you couldn't really blame her. Now she was like a nervous racehorse at the starting gate. She couldn't wait for the signal to bolt.

But her father had other ideas. "A couple of nice strong boys can go, Sylvie. I don't want you wandering around in this storm by yourself."

"I won't be wandering. I'll be going straight for help. Do not pass Go. Do not collect two hundred dollars," Sylvie said, with a trace of annoyance. "And may I remind you about my seven-day solo in the woods in Maine last spring? No tent, no food except what I caught or gathered myself. Any nice strong boys here who can make that claim?"

Jen laughed, despite the gravity of their situation. "I'll go with you," she found herself saying, before she even knew the words were out of her mouth. Well, why not? What good was it going to do to stay here, chattering like a set of wind-up false teeth and worrying about Dawson and Joey? At least another hike would warm her up. "I can't say I've spent a week in the woods. Or a night, even. But how bad could a walk in the woods be?"

Sylvie laughed too. She looked at her father. "Dad?"

He thought for a moment.

"You know it's the fastest way we're going to get help," she said. "I've taken these trails a million times."

"I don't like it, but okay," Dr. McCann finally consented. "Be careful, sweetheart. You too, young lady. Make sure you've got good waterproof gear on, and the first-aid kit."

"Right, Dad," said Sylvie.

"Jennifer," Jen said. She turned to Sylvie. "Jen Lindley. Ready when you are."

Chapter 7

"I'm scared, Dawson." Joey sat down on a log and took a few long, slow breaths. Her pulse was racing, and her heart beat wildly. They were hopelessly lost. They'd passed that skeleton tree two more times, and each time they were more exhausted and more desperate.

"Come on, Joe," Dawson urged. "We're not going to find everyone else by sitting here in the rain."

"We're not going to find them going around in circles, either," Joey said.

Dawson sat down next to her. "Believe it or not, I can't disagree with you."

"I believe it," Joey said miserably.

"Well, at least we're getting along better than we were a little while ago," Dawson joked weakly.

Joey was too frightened to muster up more than a sigh that was lost on the wind.

So Dawson wished they had never kissed. So what? What difference did it make what was going on between her and Dawson if they perished here, like Captain Sam and Maria Hallett?

Jen could feel her leg muscles as she worked to keep up with Sylvie. "Don't you think we should look for Dawson and Joey?" she asked. Sylvie hadn't been kidding about taking the fastest route off Billings Island. She plowed ahead through the heavy rain, barely glancing right or left. "What if they went down one of these other trails?" Jen said, pointing to a narrower, more overgrown path that led off into the woods.

"Jen, there are dozens of trails all over Billings Island. We can't go down all of them on a wild-goose chase." Sylvie looked back at Jen. She must have caught her worried frown. "It's not that I don't want to find them, Jen. But the best thing is to get some official help as fast as we can. They'll send a search party out right away for your friends. I promise."

"Well, I suppose, but what if . . . I don't know, what if they're in some kind of trouble out there?"

"My dad scared you with his hypothermia and all that, didn't he?" Sylvie shook her head. "It would have to get an awful lot colder, and the wind would have to get way worse for anything even remotely bad to happen. People who climb Mount Everest get hypothermia. People who fall through holes in iced-over lakes get hypothermia."

"That's really comforting," Jen deadpanned.

"No, really. They'll be okay. Secret: my dad's one

of the world's biggest babies. Needs his mug of warm milk before bed. Wears pajamas with pictures of little fishies on them. Scout's honor. He just didn't want to wait out there in that storm all wet and cold," Sylvie said.

Jen giggled.

"Besides, your friends have each other. You can keep pretty warm huddled together."

Jen stopped giggling. For one insane moment, she felt a tug of envy thinking of Joey, lost and alone with Dawson—and snuggled up next to him. In front of her, Sylvie picked up the pace.

"You ever consider a career as a personal trainer?" Jen broke into a jog to keep up with Sylvie. "You're a runner, aren't you?"

"Cross-country," Sylvie said. "And swim team. Even if certain people think I look too fat to be an athlete," she added, her characteristic humor gone.

"Oh." Jen frowned. "Sylvie, Pacey can definitely be a moron when he wants to be, but I really don't think he meant what he said."

"But he said it." Sylvie's voice wavered.

Jen was silent. What could she answer? That Pacey was ashamed to be getting friendly with someone who didn't fit into a size 4 cheerleader's outfit?

But all thoughts of Pacey's idiocy were vaporized as a bolt of lightning came hurtling right toward them. Jen gave a start of fright. Sylvie stopped in her tracks.

Boom! The lightning found a massive evergreen just ahead. *Crack!* The tree split with the sound of an explosive going off. Jen felt Sylvie grab her arm and pull her back several feet on the puddle-soaked trail.

"Don't move!" Sylvie yelled. It was the first time Jen had heard fear in Sylvie's voice.

You could hear the groan of the wood, as the evergreen went over. Jen watched, frozen. Crashing through the branches of the other trees, it fell. Down, down, down . . . It seemed to happen in slow motion. A final dance. Until it smashed to the ground. Right where Jen had been standing a moment earlier.

A cry escaped her lips. The huge tree lay across the path, blocking it entirely with its massive trunk and spiney branches.

"Are you okay?" Sylvie asked.

Jen nodded. "You?"

"Yeah. A little shaky," Sylvie admitted.

The two girls trod a makeshift path around the newly fallen tree. Okay, so Dawson and Joey might be getting too cozy to die of hypothermia. But that didn't mean there weren't other dangers waiting in the storm.

Dawson and Joey crashed through the wet brush. "There's something up ahead!" Dawson said. His flagging spirits were sparked by a glimmer of promise. "See? That patch of gray through the trees, there?"

"Sort of." Joey squinted through the rain. "Maybe it's just more trees, Dawson." She sounded uneasy. "I don't know about going off the path. We're lost enough as it is."

"We're so lost we can't get more lost," Dawson

reasoned. "Come on, Joe. There's something there. I can definitely see it." He plowed ahead, feeling a renewed energy. Joey didn't protest. He could hear her wading through the wet, low undergrowth behind him. "Maybe we managed to find our way off Billings Island." His excitement swelled. "Look, Joe. Tell me you don't see it. Right there."

"Well . . . hey, yeah! Two o'clock!" A note of hope rose in Joey's voice. "Oh, my God. Do you think—"

"I think it's a house!" Dawson moved faster. As he got closer, he was more and more certain. A solid gray wall loomed behind a stand of evergreen trees. He broke into a jog. A wall, and a slant of shingled roof peeped through at him. "It *is* a house! Tell me it's not a mirage, Joe!"

He weaved his way through the grove of trees and into the small clearing beyond them. And there it was. His energy sagged. He felt a pinch of disappointment.

"It's not a mirage," Joey said, coming to a halt next to him. "A mirage would have four complete walls and an entire roof."

"And a hot shower and a hot meal," Dawson added. He surveyed the broken-down shell of a shack. One side was almost completely open to the elements. The other side still had a patchy covering of worn gray shingles, with more than a few bare spots. Dawson could see a few beer cans and waterlogged bottles on the floor of the open end. Rain pounded what was left of the shack, and he got the feeling that what remained of it could come down any second.

"Doesn't look like we made it off Billings Island," Joey said dispiritedly.

"I guess not," Dawson concurred. There wasn't even a hint of path leading from the abandoned hut, let alone a road or a telephone pole or a faraway light beckoning through the trees in the distance.

"Which means one thing, Dawson. You know where we are?" Joey stared at the dilapidated walls as she spoke. "That girl Sylvie was telling us about this place. The only house left on Billings Island. The place she called . . ."

Her sentence trailed off. Dawson felt a flush of embarrassment. He sneaked a look at Joey. She dropped her gaze toward the muddy ground. "The love shack." He finished her sentence quietly.

In his movie script this would have would have been the perfect scene. Hero and heroine stumble across a romantic little shelter from the storm. They know it's fate. All is forgiven. They rush inside and wait out the storm in each other's arms.

But in real life it never worked out that neatly. How had Dawson managed to miss that, up until so recently? Now he and Joey stood, silent and uncomfortable. Once upon a time he'd been able to read Joey like a favorite storybook. He'd known just what she was thinking, just when she was thinking it. Now . . . well, Dawson couldn't even count on a clear picture of his own feelings, let alone Joey's.

His hero would have scooped Joey up in his arms. Carried her over that long-vanished threshold.

Instead Dawson had to wonder whether Joey would prefer to battle the storm rather than seek shelter with him inside that place. And he was still angry enough with her to hesitate.

So there they were, with the rain rolling in cold drops down their faces. A standoff. "Well?" Dawson finally asked softly.

Joey shrugged, still not meeting his eyes. "Well, it's better than standing out here in the rain," she said. "If there's any place dry in there, I guess."

"Should we look inside?" Dawson asked tentatively.

But they both stood rooted to the spot, like a couple of trees.

"It's just what the kids around here call it," Dawson said.

"Right. It doesn't mean anything," Joey responded. "It's just a place to wait out the storm."

So much for carrying her over the threshold. They approached the open end of the love shack and stepped in, keeping a respectable distance from each other.

Chapter 8

Pacey felt like the biggest heel in the commonwealth of Massachusetts. Maybe on the whole East Coast. He was soaked to the bone, chilled, miserable—and he deserved every wet, horrible minute of it.

He huddled with the other Capesiders in the nook in the dunes where they'd had their picnic. But the valley of sand that had been so cozy earlier was no match for the violent rain and winds. Pacey tucked his face into the crook of his arm until a particularly bad gust had blown over. Otherwise the sand would have chafed his face like sandpaper. It was certainly a lesson in the power of nature. More of one than anyone on this trip had signed up for.

"Witter, we could use a few of your dumb jokes about now," said Cliff Elliot.

"Sorry, Cliff. I'm afraid my jokes have just about

dried up. At least something has," he added after a suitable beat.

A few people laughed weakly.

"Yup, that was a dumb one," Cliff said. "But I give you an A for effort."

" 'Effort' doesn't start with an A," Pacey said. "But that's what happens when you let people into school on football scholarships, I guess."

The laughter was a bit heartier that time.

"Okay, I guess in emergencies I can deal with the joke being on me," Cliff said.

"Can't spell, but they sure are heroic," Pacey cracked.

"I hate to break it to you guys," said Marla Adams, "but the real heroes are the two girls who went to get help."

"Yeah," Abby spoke up, taking a break from her overplayed shivering and moaning, "and you didn't see any football stars or class clowns volunteering to go."

Pacey felt his misery come crashing back, accompanied by a fresh clap of thunder. "Abby, if it would do any good, I'd sacrifice you to the god of storms faster than you can say 'royal pain in the butt,' " he said, "but the truth is . . . you're right about who the heroes are. And I'm just sorry I let anyone embarrass me into calling one of them . . . names." He turned and looked at Cliff. "If she *was* trying to get to know me, I'm flattered, okay?"

Cliff put his hands up in the storm-battered air. "Okay, okay. Sure. No one said you shouldn't be."

Another herculean gust of wind blew across the dunes. Pacey tucked his face into his arm again. It was one thing to tell Cliff and Abby and the others how sorry he was. Getting Sylvie to forgive him was another matter.

"I never, ever, in a million years would have thought a rainy parking lot full of puddles could look so beautiful," Jen said exuberantly. Her legs ached from walking, and there wasn't a cell in her body that wasn't waterlogged, but the cold and fear were being edged out by proud triumph.

"Beauty is in the eye of the beholder," Sylvie answered. "And thank Mom Nature that we made it here to behold this place. Put it there," she added, holding her hands out to Jen for a high ten.

Jen slapped her wet, frozen hands against Sylvie's, then reeled her in for a big hug. "We made it!" she said jubilantly. She released Sylvie and took a better look around. "Wait a minute," she said, her jubilation dampened as she took in the totally, completely deserted parking lot and the narrow blacktop road that led away from it. "We made it where? Looks like we're still out here by ourselves."

"Not to worry," Sylvie assured her. "There are houses right around that curve in the road. Summer residents, mostly, but an old teacher of mine lives a few minutes from here."

"An old teacher? What are we waiting for?" Jen and Sylvie set out across the parking lot, their shoes oozing water against the hard surface of the road as they nearly ran the final stretch.

They followed the curve in the road, and a huge modern house loomed into view, all sleek wood and huge windows and a wraparound deck. But the many windows of the house were dark. "That's not your teacher's house, is it?" Jen asked.

Sylvie shook her head. "People from Boston, I think. Come up here on weekends. Not the next one, either." They passed an oversize saltbox with a hefty ship's anchor decorating the yard. That house, too, was dark.

And then, down the road a few more paces, a tiny gray-shingled cabin came into view. Yellow shutters. A vintage VW Rabbit in the driveway. And the wonderful, alluring, welcoming sight of electric lights on inside. Civilization! Jen felt her mood soar. The house was a beacon. It was an oasis. It was . . . the finish line.

She sprinted. So did Sylvie. Out of breath, they knocked on the door of the little house. Sylvie's old teacher, in her sweet, modest home, whipping up mugs of steaming hot chocolate for her former student and friend. Dripping on the doorstep, Jen could almost feel the warming drink going through her now.

Footsteps sounded inside. The door was opened.

And Jen found herself staring up at a tall, handsome, dark-haired, brown-eyed, world-class babe.

"Hi, Mr. Yarrow. Remember me? Sylvie McCann? Third period art? Jim McCann's daughter?" Sylvie said, her words toppling over each other in a rush.

This was the "old teacher"? Jen felt her heart doing a funny kind of lurch.

"Sylvie. Sylvie McCann. Sure. What brings you . . . My God, you're drenched. What in the world . . . ? Look, come on out of the rain, both of you." The hunk stepped back to let Sylvie and Jen through.

"Mr. Yarrow, we just walked all the way from the far end of Billings Island," Sylvie explained with urgency, as they entered the house. "My dad—he took a group of students out on a whale watch. We got stranded out there. Two people are lost. The rest of them are waiting for us to get help."

Mr. Yarrow put a hand to his head. "Whoa, Sylvie. You're telling me there's a bunch of people shipwrecked out there? In this weather?"

Sylvie nodded. "I'm sorry to just show up on your doorstep . . . Oh, by the way, this is Jen."

"Jen. Hi." In the soft light of the tiny foyer, those brown eyes met her gaze and held it for a moment.

"Um, hi," Jen managed. "We're dripping all over your floor."

"Please. Talk about a visit from an old student . . . This sure is dramatic. Look, don't worry about getting anything wet," he told Jen. "In fact, why don't you both go dry up in the bathroom? Down the hall, first door on your right. Let me call over to the police station this second. Get someone moving right away. Then I'll find you something dry to put on."

Jen watched the babe hurry off to call for help. She and Sylvie headed for the little bathroom. Bumping elbows, they quickly and gratefully shed their sopping clothes and wrapped themselves in big, soft towels.

"That's your old teacher?" Jen whispered as they piled their dripping clothes in the sink.

"Well, 'old' as in he used to be my teacher. Not

'old' as in . . . well, you know. He was actually an assistant teacher when I was still going to school here. I think he's the main art teacher now. Cute, huh?"

Jen laughed. She was dry. She was warming up. Help was on the way for her classmates. And Sylvie's teacher was . . . very nice. "Worth walking every single stormy mile," she said.

It wasn't much of a love shack. It wasn't much of a shack at all. The floorboards were warped and rotting, and the remaining part of the roof had as many holes as Swiss cheese. The interior walls were gone, and the posts and beams that had supported them stood like ghosts. The rubble of a fireplace and chimney left scars on the closed end of the house. Everything was a dirty, dark gray, to match the sky through the open window frames.

Joey could think of about a million places that would have been more romantic. Love shack? Not a chance. They were out of the rain and wind, true, but it wasn't exactly warm and inviting in here.

She and Dawson had staked out one of the few dry spots under the largest, safest-looking stretch of roof.

"What a dive, huh?" Joey said. "Wonder how long it's been since you could get a fire going in the fireplace."

Dawson eyed the pile of bricks and rubble. "We just have to think warm, I guess. Think of this place in better times. Cozy little house. New, fresh. All hammered up dry and tight. The smell of pine still wafting from the floorboards and the walls. The fireplace blazing with a crackling fire . . ."

Joey followed his gaze to the ruins of the fireplace. Dawson could set a scene, no denying that. For one moment, Joey actually managed to see the welcome flames, to hear them licking the logs. For one moment she even felt a little warmer.

"Two people, safe against the storm," Dawson said, nodding. "Two people . . ." His voice trailed off.

Joey looked at him. Their eyes met. She looked away. Two people. Making sure to keep some air between them.

She felt ice-cold again. She shivered. It had been a mistake, kissing Dawson. It had never happened. Dawson had said so himself. No wonder Joey had felt so uncomfortable around him all day. She'd been right on the money to hold back her feelings. To be wary. To be . . . leery . . . of Leery. She gave a short, hard laugh at the pun she'd made in her head.

"Joey?" Dawson asked.

"Huh? Oh, nothing," Joey said quickly.

"Not going to let me in on the joke? I could use a laugh right about now."

"Forget about it, Dawson."

"Okay. Fine. Fine, Joey." Dawson sounded as cold as Joey felt. "Maybe you'd rather I didn't say anything at all."

Joey felt a tickle of remorse. "Look, I didn't mean to be mean, Dawson. It's just that there's really nothing here to laugh about," she said. "Not the way it is now." She sighed. Her voice softened. "So why don't we just go back to imagining this place the way it might have been?"

Dawson let out a long breath. "Well . . . it *is* a great setting for a movie. You have to give me that."

Movies. Always movies. Dawson was great at movies. Not so great at reality. And this was reality. Very unfortunately.

Then again, dreaming up stories for what might have been was at least as good a way to pass the time as any. And an awful lot better than dwelling on their current situation.

Fire in the fireplace . . . the house in better times . . . Who could have lived in this place once upon a time, and why? Joey put her imagination to work.

Chapter 9

Jen sank back into the deep, soft sofa pillows, blissfully dry and toasty in the oversize gray sweatshirt and sweatpants Mr. Yarrow had lent her. He'd also brought out a warm down quilt, which she and Sylvie were sharing as a lap blanket. The house was warm and comfortable, and even the rain now sounded friendly, drumming against the roof like a lulling song.

Jen let out a sigh of contentment.

"Mmm. I know what you mean," Sylvie said, next to her.

It couldn't have been cozier inside this house. The blond wood walls were hung with their host's large, bright paintings—vibrant abstract shapes, charged with movement and color. The wide-plank floors were bare throughout most of the room—stark and elegant—but a few decorative throw rugs warmed the space up visually. The furniture was limited to a few simple pieces, giving the smallish room a deceptively spacious and airy feeling. But the wall-sized bookshelves were crammed with books, and every flat surface was a showcase for the textures and colors of found objects—driftwood and sea glass, bottle tops and marbles, polished stones in a wooden bowl, a silver saltshaker.

You could fall for the guy just looking around his living room, Jen thought. Or maybe she was getting carried away by the euphoria of simply being snug and comfortable and sitting in one place, with the rain outside, where it belonged.

All of a sudden, she felt guilty. Everyone else from Capeside was still out there, freezing and frightened, with no shelter from the pounding elements. And Dawson and Joey—no one even knew where they were. Jen felt her cozy happiness drenched by worry.

But the babe was smiling as he returned to the room. A handsome, irresistible lopsided smile. "Okay, Sylvie, Chief Rosenthal is on the job. You remember him?"

Sylvie nodded. "The police chief in town," she explained to Jen.

"They're getting the cots and blankets set up in the high school gym right away," their host filled them in. "Standard hurricane procedure around here. No big deal. They'll send a bus out to the Billings Island parking lot. The bus isn't exactly equipped to get down those dirt trails, but they'll ferry your party off the Island in smaller groups. They're mobilizing the ATVs for their mission."

"A TV?" Jen asked.

"ATVs," Sylvie said. "All-terrain vehicles."

"Jeeps to you," added the babe.

"Oh. Uh-duh," Jen said. "We've got those in New York to navigate the potholes. Well . . . thanks so much for all your help."

"Yeah, thanks, Mr. Yarrow," Sylvie said.

"Steve. Please. School's closed for inclement weather. Rain day. I get to lose the Mister. I've never really felt entirely comfortable with it. I mean, when I started teaching your class, Sylvie, I think I was closer in age to the students than to most of the other teachers."

Sylvie nodded. "Okay, then. Well, thanks . . . Steve," she said a bit awkwardly.

Steve laughed. "My pleasure." He showered Sylvie with *that* smile—and then turned it on Jen. "My pleasure," he repeated.

Jen felt her cheeks grow pink. "We're just lucky you were right here. And our wet classmates are going to be happy about it, too." A roll of thunder sounded outside.

"Have no fear. Your classmates are as good as settled in old Newcomb High," Steve said.

"Wait. How about Dawson and Joey?" Jen asked, the spell of Steve broken for a moment.

"Who?" Steve asked. "Oh, the two guys who are lost? I told Chief Rosenthal about them. He's putting together a search party. Calling on some of the Seashore rangers who know the island best."

"Oh," Jen said. "Well, let's hope they find them fast. They're not guys, though." She found herself correcting Steve's mistake. "Well, one of them is.

Dawson. Dawson's a guy." She heard the silly way her explanation was coming out and she gave a little laugh. Yup. Dawson was a guy. An image flashed through her head of the first time they had kissed—on her grandmother's front lawn. How sweet he'd been. How nice it had felt in his arms. Then the image shifted: Dawson's bedroom. Dawson racing out—racing after Joey, and leaving Jen behind. "Joey," she said softly, "she's not a guy. She's a girl." A fact that Dawson finally seemed to be waking up to.

"Oh," Steve said. "Well, okay. A girl and a guy. They'll be all right, Jen. The rangers will find them."

His voice snapped Jen out of her reverie. Girl, guy . . . nothing was simple. But efforts were being made to find Dawson and Joey. That was the important thing. Soon they'd be safe. And warm. And dry.

Jen watched Steve ease himself into the overstuffed armchair across from her. He smiled. She felt the coziness of his house start to work its charm again. And the owner of the house was pretty charming, too. She smiled back at him. Dawson would be okay. Besides, when she looked at Steve, Dawson seemed very far away . . . wherever he was.

Dawson pulled his knees up to his chest and wrapped his arms around them, but it was impossible to get anywhere close to comfortable. You could imagine as roaring a fire as you wanted, in that useless wreck of a fireplace. It didn't change the fact that his jeans were wet and his fingers were numb.

But Joey had taken his advice to heart, and was off and running on a game of What If. "I got it!

What if this was once that pirate's wife's house?" she was wondering out loud. "Maria Hallett's house. What do you think, Dawson?"

"I think she was out of luck if the fireplace wasn't in better shape," Dawson joked feebly.

"No, really," Joey insisted. "I mean, she had to go somewhere after they banished her from town. And didn't that Sylvie girl say Sam and Maria got married on Billings Island? This was their special place, you know? Nighttime in the apple orchard, moonlight, all that. So why wouldn't she have come here when she was waiting for Sam? And after . . . when she and her baby were all alone? This was where her happy memories were. This was where she could remember what it was like to be with him."

"I won't tell anyone you're a hopeless romantic, Joey." Dawson laughed.

Joey gave an embarrassed shrug. "Romantic? With that poor woman's husband down at the bottom of the ocean? Maybe it would've been romantic if Sam hadn't drowned. I don't exactly see where being a single mother in a dump like this is so romantic."

"Okay, then. So let's do a rewrite." Dawson really couldn't resist joining in the game, no matter how wet he was. "Maria Hallett didn't live here without Captain Sam," he said. "The big secret behind the legend is that he didn't drown. He sneaked back here and came right home to Maria and their baby."

"Wait a minute, Dawson. Legend or no legend, the fact is that the *Whydah* was real. Captain Sam was real. The *Whydah* went down, and he went down with her. Because everyone knows, a ship is the captain's real mistress. The *Whydah* was the one he died for. Not Maria."

"Okay, so I'm taking a little dramatic license here. A person's allowed. I'm directing this version. I'm in control."

Joey raised an eyebrow. "Highly doubtful, Dawson. You don't even have dry clothes, let alone control."

Dawson grimaced. "Don't remind me. You want to talk about wet and cold, or you want to talk about Sam and Maria?"

"Sam and Maria," Joey said immediately. "Definitely Sam and Maria."

"Good. So the *Whydah* did go down," Dawson said. "But Captain Sam managed to get to shore. Secretly. And Maria was waiting. She'd been watching the whole awful thing, just like Sylvie told us, but in her heart of hearts she knew Sam wasn't dying. They were connected. They were soul mates. She would have felt it if his spirit had gone from the earth."

"Did someone say hopeless romantic?" Joey asked.

Dawson ignored her. He was on a roll. He could see the story through his camera lens. "Picture it, Joey. Sam pulling himself ashore. Not dead, but almost. Not drowned, but almost. He half crawls, half drags himself up the beach and over the first rise of dune, out of the reach of the angry ocean. What's left of his clothes are tattered and ripped. His face and body are bruised and swollen. He collapses right where he is. He can't go any farther.

"And then, her touch. He thinks he's dreaming. He thinks he's swallowed too much seawater and he's hallucinating. He thinks he died and he's in heaven. But it's really Maria and their tiny baby. They have a tender reunion. She brings him back here to this cabin and nurses him to health. By then they know that they're going to stay here. Away from the townspeople who cast her out. No one to punish him for thievery on the high seas. No one to punish her for falling in love with the bad boy of the Atlantic. . . ."

Joey was nodding now, taking the ride with him. "They've left the problems of the world behind. . . . You know, Dawson, you've got something there. No fathers behind bars. No broken families. No bad reps among the neighbors."

"See? I thought you'd like it. Nothing can touch them here. It's just the two of them. Well, the three of them, actually. I can see them. The baby's sleeping in a little wooden cradle. Captain Sam's fixing his fishing gear. He fishes for their meals now—a simpler kind of treasure."

Joey rolled her eyes.

"Too corny? Well, we won't spell it out. You'll just see Sam sitting on one of those long, hard benches they used to have in their houses, mending his net. She's weaving her cloth. Focus in on her fingers—so long and elegant—turning threads into beautiful fabric. Camera pulls back and we see her, smiling and content, her—"

"Can we fast-forward this part?" Joey cut him off. "Her hair as blond as sunshine, eyes as blue as the water . . . yes, okay, go on."

Dawson stopped instead. He felt a cold drop of surprise. In fact, he'd been picturing Maria Hallett with dark hair and brown eyes. He hadn't even been fully aware of it until this second. But the Maria Hallett of his movie fantasies looked very much like—

"Joey?" he said. He looked at her. Her pretty face, set so hard. Desire and frustration welled up in him.

"Yeah, Dawson?"

"Never mind, Joey," he said. "My story's over. Final act."

He'd tried with her. He really had. He'd tried on the boat. He'd tried at the picnic. He'd tried on the nature walk. He was reminded of the Dr. Seuss book his parents used to read him when he was little. "Not on a box, not with a fox, not with a mouse, not in a house . . ." Or at least it went something like that.

He breathed out a long gray plume of visible breath. And certainly not in this cold, damp shell of a house.

Jen and Sylvie told their story over again to Chief Rosenthal and three other policemen. "The whole full-time winter police force of this town," Steve had told an incredulous Jen, before Rosenthal and his men arrived.

A four-person police force. Barely enough for one subway train.

"But we do get some serious crimes around here," Steve had said. "You should read the police blotter in the local paper. Saturday, ten P.M. Loud music reported on Gull Way. Hey, guys, nothing like a wild Saturday night. Sunday, noon. Cat stuck up in tree."

Jen had been laughing then, but now the policemen were dead serious. "How many in your group? How many students? How many adults? The two who are missing—can you give us a complete description? What were they wearing? They were last seen when?"

Jen and Sylvie did their best to answer the questions. Every misstep meant more time out in the storm for their friends and classmates. Every bit of helpful information could mean a quick rescue.

Rescue and the shelter of the school gym. Jen felt reluctant. The gym might be a welcome haven for her storm-beaten classmates, but Jen didn't have the slightest desire to swap this cozy sanctuary for a big, loud, crowded school gymnasium. Okay, if she was honest with herself, maybe her reluctance had less to do with location than with present company. She liked Steve. They couldn't have knocked on a better door. And she wasn't ready to say good-bye to him.

Her genie-in-a-bottle came in the form of big salt-and-pepper-haired Chief Rosenthal. "Sylvie, I'd like you to come with us, since you know the Billings Island trails, and show us where the boat is, and where the missing two were last seen. Jennifer, if you don't mind, and if Steve doesn't mind, I'm going to ask him to take you over to the school. We've got a large group stranded out there, and we need all the space we've got in our vehicles to bring them on in."

Jen smiled sweetly at Chief Rosenthal. "That's perfectly fine with me," she told him. "If it's okay with Steve." She looked over at him and felt herself blush.

He met her gaze and answered her smile with his own. "No problem at all," he said. "Whenever you're ready, I'll take you over there."

"Sylvie?" Chief Rosenthal asked.

"Ready, Chief," she said. "Oh, Mr. Ya— Steve, I still have your sweats on."

"Keep them. I'll send your other clothes over with Jen, when they come out of the dryer."

The police chief and his men lost no time getting moving. Jen gave Sylvie a hug. "Good luck," she said.

"You too," Sylvie whispered meaningfully.

And then Jen was alone with Steve.

Chapter 10

Joey felt like a drowned fruit slice at the bottom of a punch bowl. She couldn't remember what it was like to be dry. The wind howled through the branches outside; the rain pounded what was left of the roof and poured down through the open spots. It was growing decidedly darker, from stormy gray afternoon to shadowy early evening. It was getting even colder in the love shack. Or at least Joey was getting colder. She rubbed her damp, sweater-covered arms hard and fast, trying to produce enough friction to generate some heat.

"Whoever it was who lived here, they better have had a monster pile of firewood," she said to Dawson.

Dawson gave an abbreviated laugh. "Maybe that's why half the house is gone. They used up the wood and went for the furniture. They used up the furniture and went to work on the walls."

Joey matched his short laugh. "I don't blame them. I'd do anything for a nice fire right now."

A giant broom of lightning split the sky over the open part of the shack. Joey instinctively reeled back from it. The thunder that followed shook the house. She let out a gasp.

Dawson gave a low whistle. "Close call. Did I hear someone say she'd do anything for a fire?"

Joey grimaced. "Careful what you wish for. Can you have a forest fire in the middle of a rainstorm?"

Dawson nodded. "Sure. I saw it in this movie about this special unit of firefighters in the Pacific Northwest."

"Fiction or documentary?" Joey asked.

"Ah, Joe, the line between fact and fiction is not a simple thing," Dawson joked.

"Yeah, well, the line between dead and alive is," Joey said, looking up at the part of the darkening sky where they'd seen the lightning.

"Some people would debate that," Dawson said.

"Maybe. I wouldn't want to personally test any of the more mystical theories at this point in my young life. So . . . you think someone's going to come find us here? Or are we going to have to go out there and walk around in circles again?"

Dawson sighed. "I don't know. Everyone else must have gotten back to the boat hours ago. You'd think they'd have sent people out looking for us right away. Too bad about the fireplace," he added. "Although even if it was brand-new, we don't have any matches to start a fire."

Joey shivered. "Dawson, weren't you ever a Boy Scout? Didn't they ever teach you how to rub two sticks together to get a spark going? Give you one of those little round badges your mom could sew on your uniform?"

"Dad," Dawson said. "Dad does the sewing, not Mom. And no, I was never a Boy Scout. You know I don't go in much for those group activities, Joe. And I don't think they have a badge for film-making."

"They don't. At least they didn't in the Brownies."

In the waning light, Joey could see Dawson shoot her a funny look. "You were a Brownie? Somehow I can't picture you in one of those uniforms, going from door to door selling cookies."

"I lasted about a week," Joey admitted. "Not the week they taught us to start a fire with two sticks, unfortunately." Her teeth were chattering.

Suddenly Dawson was unzipping his jacket and wriggling out of it.

"What are you doing?" Joey asked.

"Here." He held the jacket out toward her. "Lose the wet sweater and put this on."

Joey shook her head. Dawson's arms were bare in his navy pocket T-shirt. "You're going to freeze, Dawson. You won't be much good at telling distracting stories if you're frozen."

Dawson shrugged. "I'm okay. I'm not as wet as you are. At least not the top half of me. Go ahead." He kept holding out the jacket.

Joey stared at it. Blue waterproof outer shell. Some kind of fuzzy, warm-looking lining. Hard to resist.

"Come on," Dawson said softly. "A peace offering, okay? An olive branch."

"You sure?" Joey asked.

Dawson nodded.

Joey shed her damp sweater and accepted the jacket. She felt better as soon as she put one arm into a sleeve. It was warm from Dawson's body. She quickly wriggled into the rest of the jacket and pulled it closed around her. "Mmm. Thanks, Dawson. This olive branch feels wonderful."

"You know, the olive branch signaled the end of the flood in the story of Noah's Ark," Dawson commented. "Maybe we'll have the same kind of luck."

"That would be nice." Dawson's jacket felt like him, smelled like him. Joey was enveloped by a deep sense of comfort. She offered Dawson a tentative smile.

He smiled back.

Dawson was a true friend, whatever else they were—or weren't—to each other, Joey thought. He had always been her friend, from the first time they'd sat out a softball game in the elementary school yard together. With all the new feelings between them, with all the complications, good and bad, with the brand-new paths on which to lose and find themselves, there was no question that Dawson was the person she could count on. The person she'd most want to be stuck with in a leaky hovel in a storm. At least if she had to be stuck at all.

The anger Joey had felt toward Dawson earlier was drying up.

It was a poor excuse for a slumber party, Pacey thought, as he surveyed the castaways. Several dozen cots had been set up in neat rows in the high school gymnasium, covered with donated sheets and army regulation blankets. Most of the crew members had swapped their wet clothes for temporary thrift shop surplus, brought over in the storm by a tiny older lady with a long white braid, who was hauling a garbage bag twice her size, stuffed with old clothes. "One outfit to a customer!" she'd parroted over and over as she rationed out the dry clothes. Pacey was decked out in orange plaid pants that were too short. His feet were bare.

Some people had done even worse. Keith Silves had gotten stuck with a fire-engine red bouclé sweater—definitely not from the men's department. But he was making the most of it, parading around patting the sweater and running his fingers through his light brown hair and telling everyone he'd bought it especially for the fishermen's ball.

Over on one side of the big room, a number of people were setting up a table with hot beverages and food. The little town had rallied generously, with home cooking and volunteers and an outpouring of support.

But the most striking thing for Pacey wasn't what was unusual about the situation. It was that in a twisted, red bouclé kind of way, everything was exactly the same as always. Kids in the same groups, the same spots, even, as they fell into at Capeside High.

Cliff and some of the other muscle champs of the school had seized the cots in the center of the boys' section of the room and were holding court. They even had a few cheerleaders on hand for a visit, and darned if Elizabeth Zath hadn't managed to find a really cute, really short little sixties retro number in that bag of hideous clothes. And she'd persuaded the lady with the white braid to hand it over. A fact that didn't seem to be lost on Cliff. Or on Pacey either, for that matter.

Jim Fretts and Brice Matthews and Janine Santos were playing some card game over in a far corner of the room—just the way they did at lunch at school, every day. Rachel Spinner had made an immediate pilgrimage to the upstairs library to borrow a book and was reading quietly on her cot. Which was in about the same place in the gym as her usual lunch spot was in the cafeteria. The burnouts—or at least the ones who'd woken up in time to make it on the field trip—were sneaking out of the gym to, well, burn out.

Business as usual.

Except that Pacey seemed to be the only one of his crowd who'd made it through the ordeal and out the other side. Dawson and Joey were still missing. Jen and Sylvie hadn't made an appearence in the gym yet either. Pacey tugged at his plaid pants, trying to get a little more coverage in the ankle department. He sat down on the edge of his hard little cot. Then he stood up again. It was going to be a long night.

Finally he lay back on his cot and tried to conjure up an image of Sylvie. Well, Sylvie's voice. Sylvie's personality, her enthusiasm, her ability to amuse. In the body of a buxom, leggy blond beauty.

It didn't work. All Pacey could see, when he shut his eyes, was Sylvie's round pink face—creased with hurt and disappointment. His eyes flew open. He sat up. And there she was. Coming in through the gym door. She looked dry enough, in a dark sweat suit she hadn't been wearing earlier. Pacey felt his pulse speed up. He stood and waved to her. She caught the motion of his arm and looked toward him. And the hurt and disappointment that she still felt were mirrored on her face all too plainly.

Pacey sank back down on his cot. He watched Sylvie make her way over to the section they'd set aside for the teachers and the staff from the Oceanographic Institute. The adults had a row of cots set up a suitably sedate distance from the students. She gave her father a big hug. They talked for a few minutes, and then Sylvie headed for the girls' section and chose an empty bed. She tested it out with her hand and then lay back on it and put up her feet.

Pacey took a deep breath of resolve. He got up and walked over to her. In his orange plaid pants.

Her expression was about as far from welcoming as it could be. "What do you want?" she said flatly. She didn't even bother to make a rude remark about his pants. Bad sign.

"I—um—I'm wondering if they found Dawson and Joey," Pacey stammered.

Sylvie didn't move a muscle except for her mouth. "Do you see them here?" she snapped. Then she seemed to soften just the tiniest bit. "The search party's out looking for them," she said.

Pacey shifted from one bare foot to the other. "Oh. Good. Well. I hope they find them soon."

Sylvie just closed her eyes. "We all hope that."

Pacey tried for a speck of humor. "I see they've

got the grown-ups quarantined on the other side of the room. Or is it us that're quarantined? That inexplicable, disgruntled teen behavior. I hear it's catching, you know."

Sylvie didn't react.

Pacey blew out a long breath. "Look, Sylvie, about before . . ." he began.

Sylvie's eyes flew open. "Look, Pacey. It's been a long day. A really long day, okay? Do me a really huge favor and just go back to your side of the room, all right?"

Pacey felt a sting of shame. He stood there for one more moment. Then he turned and retreated with his proverbial tail between the legs of his orange plaid pants.

Chapter 11

Jen got that mug of steaming hot chocolate, after all. And it was every bit as good as the cup she'd dreamed up at the hands of some nonexistent old lady teacher.

"The secret is steamed milk and Mexican chocolate," Steve said. He had a crackling fire going in the fireplace, and they were sitting cross-legged on the floor in front of it. The hum of the dryer sounded faintly from the other room. Jen figured her wet clothes had dried long ago, but she was in no hurry to confirm that fact. That would only mean it was time to change back into them and head for the high school. Steve didn't seem too focused on the progress of the dry cycle, either.

The flames licked at the logs, and Jen could feel the delicious warmth on her face. "So you're a big-city transplant, like me," Steve commented.

"Really? Are you a New Yorker? I mean, were you?" Jen felt a jolt of surprise. Maybe it was the aura of peace and tranquility in Steve's little house. New York seemed like another universe right now.

"I was for a while," Steve said. "I went to art school there. Lived in a one-bedroom apartment with three roommates."

"Sounds . . . cozy."

"Too cozy. But we had fun, in an *Animal House* kind of way."

"*Animal House?*" Jen asked.

"You know, vintage John Belushi," Steve explained.

"Oh. A movie buff," Jen said. Another movie buff. Maybe it was something about *her.* She seemed to be a magnet for them.

"Yeah, well, there isn't that much to do around here," Steve said. "Especially in the winter. I have to confess I've probably seen every movie in the video store a few hundred times or so." He took a sip of his own hot chocolate. "It's not every day that I get a lovely shipwrecked visitor at my door."

Jen smiled. "Thanks. I guess I'll take that as a compliment."

"You should," Steve flirted back.

Jen felt happy embarrassment. "So, um . . . where did you live before New York? Where are you originally from?"

"Boston. Brookline, actually—right outside Boston. My family used to spend summers here when I was growing up."

"And your parents are still in Brookline?"

"My mom is. She's a pediatrician. My dad's not alive anymore."

"I'm sorry," Jen offered.

"Yeah. Me too," Steve said simply.

"Brothers and sisters?"

"One older sister. She's a graphic designer in Boston. Watch out, Jen, because *you're* going to be answering *my* questions next," he added lightly.

Jen laughed. "Fair enough. But humor me through a few more questions, okay? It's not every day that I get shipwrecked at the door of some tall, dark, mysterious stranger," she said, borrowing Steve's words.

He laughed, too. "Fire away. The more you know, the less I'm a stranger."

"Right." Jen nodded. "So you moved up here after you graduated from art school?"

Steve nodded. "More time, more space. It started out as voluntary exile. Then it started feeling like home. I don't know—I needed to slow down or something. A lot of partying in New York. A lot of energy on all kinds of things—energy that I wanted to try to channel into my painting. Does that make sense?"

"Definitely." Jen felt a wave of recognition. Of course her exile hadn't exactly been voluntary. But there were other similarities. "You wanted to slow down."

"Exactly." Steve flashed that gorgeous lopsided smile.

"And has it worked?"

"There's a lot I miss about city life. The museums and galleries. The restaurants. The people-watching." He shrugged. "And I don't always feel like I fit in here. But . . . you make your own sense of belonging anywhere you go. It's definitely beautiful enough here. Stark in the winter, but with this minimalist kind of grace. All ocean and sky and open stretches of marshy land." He paused. "It's easier here, too. My paycheck goes farther, which means more art supplies, basically. And more room to paint."

"Looks like you've been busy," Jen said. "I like your work." She sipped at her hot chocolate as she studied the collage over the fireplace—torn fragments of black-and-white newspaper photos, against bold planes of oil paint on glass.

"Thanks. That's a pretty recent one. I'm getting more into using different kinds of materials," Steve said. "I'm having a show next summer at a gallery in Provincetown, on the tip of the Cape. I don't know—maybe a New York gallery's next, if I'm lucky."

Jen nodded. "So . . . you'd think about moving back there?"

Steve was pensive. "Truth is, I'm pretty happy here. I like my teaching job a lot. And I do some work over the summer for one of my buddies who does carpentry and construction. Bang a few nails, you know. It's a living. I've turned the garage into a great studio. Catch some good waves on my boogie board when it's warm. Get out on my bike most days. Present weather excepted. I don't know, really. I think I may be here for the long haul." Steve looked at Jen and held her gaze. "Only problem is it can get kind of lonely sometimes," he said softly.

Jen looked into his brown eyes and didn't look away. The more she got to know about Steve, the more she liked him. She had the perfect solution to his problem: let the dryer keep going forever. She wouldn't mind waiting and keeping Steve company.

When Pacey saw Sylvie leaving the gym, he was ready. He followed her down the hallway at a distance. She turned in at the ladies' room. He positioned himself outside the door and waited. When she came out, he made his move.

"Sylvie," he said, taking a step toward her.

Sylvie gave a start of alarm. "Oh." The alarm turned to annoyance. "It's you. What are you doing, practicing your stalking skills?"

"Apologizing skills," Pacey said contritely.

Sylvie was quiet for a moment. Her mouth turned down at the corners. "You tried your apologizing skills already," she finally said. "You got an F as in Forget it."

"If at first you don't succeed . . . ?" Pacey said meekly.

"You succeeded," Sylvie said flatly. "In making sure I knew exactly how you *really* felt."

"Except I didn't," Pacey protested. "I succeeded in getting embarrassed in front of a couple of losers, and I acted like a loser too."

"No argument there." Sylvie pressed her lips together.

"I didn't mean what I said. I think you're . . . a really great person."

"Great as in grand as in big," Sylvie said tightly. "Huge."

"No," Pacey said.

"A whale."

Pacey winced. "I'm really, really sorry."

"So am I, Pacey. I thought we were really hitting it off."

"I thought so too."

"So that's why you decided to make me the butt—the big butt—of your joke. So to speak," Sylvie added with a soft, derisive laugh.

"That's not funny," Pacey said quietly.

Sylvie's expression was instantly severe. "No. No, it's not. That's really my point."

"I didn't mean to hurt you," Pacey tried.

"Then what did you mean?"

He let out a long, unhappy breath. "Look, Sylvie, the truth is, I think I kind of had a thing for you the second I heard your voice on the boat."

"Then you saw me. Be a big man, Pacey. Admit it. You were disappointed."

Pacey shut his eyes, then opened them again. "Okay. Yes. I was a little disappointed. But that's because I'm a moron, Sylvie. One of the moronic sex. We have this inability to think with the brain that's in our head, sometimes, and—well, we have another brain that's not so smart all right?"

"And it does about seventy-five percent of the thinking," Sylvie said.

Pacey arched an eyebrow. "Is that all?"

Sylvie didn't cave in to a smile.

"So okay, maybe I had this stupid fantasy that you were going to look exactly like someone from *Baywatch.*"

"I did. I looked like the whale."

"Would you stop saying that word?"

"Why? It's going around and around and around in my head, Pacey. And I have you to thank for it."

Pacey took a deep breath. "Sylvie, would you just listen to me? Just hear what I'm trying to tell you. Maybe you didn't look like Pamela Anderson, okay? But the more I talked to you, the more I liked you. When we were walking around Billings Island after the picnic I—I was thinking about kissing you."

"Me or Pam?" Sylvie challenged.

Should he tell her the truth: you, but in a Pam-like body? Pacey hesitated. And his hesitation was as much of an answer as Sylvie needed.

"I'm going back to the gym, Pacey," she said. "To my little cot. By myself. I suggest you do the same thing."

"And feel your anger across the room all night?" Pacey shook his head. "Maybe I'll just go out and take a walk on those dunes with that ghost. Keep that Maria girl company out there."

"Fine," Sylvie said tonelessly. She turned on her heel and headed up the hall toward the gym.

Chapter 12

"Better?" Dawson asked.

Joey nodded. "Not exactly a tropical paradise, but the iceberg effect's wearing off." Her jeans were starting to dry—at least they'd gone from wet to damp, and Dawson's jacket was definitely working. But Dawson was chillin' now, and not in the good sense. Joey could see the goose bumps on his arms. "Here, why don't you take it back now?" She put her hand on the zipper, even though she couldn't bear to part with the jacket.

"It's okay," Dawson said. "Keep it on for a few more minutes. Hey, I can handle it," he added, in a mock-macho tone. "John Wayne, Burt Lancaster, Bruce Willis, Arnold Schwarzenegger."

"Woody Allen." Joey laughed, then added sincerely, "Thanks, Dawson."

"Any time, Joe. Really." She could hear that Dawson meant it, too.

They were quiet for a few minutes. But it was a different kind of silence than it had been for most of the day. They shared this wordlessness comfortably. It wasn't a wall between them. The rain drummed on the roof and the stretches of floor that were bare to the sky.

"Dawson?" Joey eventually said.

"Uh-huh?"

"Dawson, I'm sorry I got you so mad, before."

Dawson shrugged.

"Friends?" Joey asked.

Dawson drew a long breath, but didn't answer. All of a sudden Joey didn't feel so comfortable with the silence anymore.

"Say something, Dawson," she implored him.

"Is that what we are? Friends? I thought we'd gotten past that particular fiction." Joey could hear the tension creeping back into Dawson's voice.

"You're saying we're not friends?" Her own tension came back.

"Joey, what is wrong with you?" Dawson's voice was barely controlled. "I just don't get it. Call me dense. Tell me I'm living in a fantasy world. I thought . . . well, I thought we had a pretty amazing thing going."

Joey bit her lip. She certainly didn't disagree with him.

"Okay, let me go out on a limb here, Joey. At least one of us had an amazing time."

Joey thought about Dawson's kisses. His awesome kisses. "Dawson . . . you may be living in a fantasy world. In fact, I know you're living in a fantasy world. But . . . I had a pretty amazing time, too. Okay?"

Dawson's voice softened. "Okay? I don't know if it's okay, Joey. You tell me. Every time I looked at you today . . . well, you went running off to the bathroom." He shook his head and gave a little laugh. "And look where it got us this time."

"See? You shouldn't have waited." Joey gave an embarrassed little laugh of her own.

"You know what I think?" Dawson asked. Joey said nothing, but he answered anyway. "I think you're scared."

"Of what?" Joey threw back defensively.

Dawson shook his head. "I don't know. Well . . . maybe I do. I was scared too, Joey. Maybe that's why we kept going around in circles with each other and never getting anywhere. I don't mean out there on those trails. I mean . . . with each other. All year. Ever since—well, whenever, Joey. Maybe we're afraid—I don't know, tell me if this makes any sense at all—we're afraid to start a fire 'cause we could get burned."

"We don't have any matches, Dawson. We established that already," Joey wisecracked.

"I'm serious, Joey." Dawson held her gaze and wouldn't let go.

Joey looked into his deep-set hazel eyes. "Okay," she said quietly. "Okay, Dawson, I know what you mean."

"And?"

"And maybe you're right." Joey wrapped her arms around herself in Dawson's jacket. "It was easier when we just went into your closet and played *Jaws.*" She couldn't even remember how it had felt to be so easy and natural with Dawson. Not to think and wonder and worry over who felt how and to whom.

"We could still go into the closet and play," Dawson whispered. He leaned closer. They were only inches apart.

Joey was overcome by that feeling again—that she absolutely had to run off downstairs or into the woods and take a few deep breaths and not have to deal with the pounding in her chest. But she willed herself to stay where she was. She didn't dare move even a muscle. Was Dawson right? Was this pure fear? "Dawson, there aren't even any walls in this sty, let alone any closets." She laughed nervously. "Besides, what about Jen?"

Dawson groaned and leaned away. "How do I get this through your head? Joey, it's over between me and Jen. At least it is for me. She and I—we're from two different worlds."

Joey rolled her eyes.

"I mean it," Dawson said. "I know where you're from, Joey. And that's part of why we understand each other the way we do."

Joey took in the serious, sensitive look on Dawson's face. Earnest. Handsome. He *was* handsome. And her pulse *was* racing. But she had to be more sure. "But what about 'opposites attract,' Dawson?" Joey had a flash of Jeremy the sax player. And Anderson Crawford. The newness, the mystery, the unknown—that had been half the fun.

"Practicing your philosophical questions for those French cafe discussions?" Dawson said, with a funny crack in his voice.

Joey passed on that one. "No, really, Dawson, I can't believe that you, of all people, are waxing poetic about the virtues of going out with someone just like you. The high school quarterback marries the star cheerleader and they start a family in the same town where they grew up. Big whoop. No one ever gets anywhere. Next scene, same as the one before. Come to think of it, Dawson, maybe Captain Sam was looking for someone different. Not just another Puritan girl in some stuffy bonnet, barefoot, pregnant, and in the kitchen. Or wherever they did the cooking in those days."

"Then who did he wind up with if it wasn't Maria?" Dawson challenged.

They were back to storytelling again. Joey felt a wave of relief—and a faint reverberation of disappointment. "Well, okay, Dawson. Suppose Sam did fake his death like you said before—swam to shore, whatever. But it wasn't Maria who was waiting for him. No. The woman on the beach was an Indian woman. The one who's still buried right here on this island. She healed Sam with local herbs and plants that the Pilgrims knew nothing about. Ministered to him with all the knowledge and traditions passed down to her and all the love blossoming between them. *She* was his real true love. Sam and the Wampanoag woman were living in this house.

Nobody bothered them because of their differences. Not so different than it is today," Joey mused.

She found herself picturing her sister Bessie and Bodie. And their plump-cheeked baby. And all the opposition they came up against every day. "Yeah, maybe Bessie and Bodie should look into fixing this place up."

"And I was starting to think of it as *our* place," Dawson joked lightly. Or was it a joke? He was moving toward her again. Closer. She could see the green and gold flecks in his hazel eyes, feel the warmth of his breath on her face. "This little house in the middle of nowhere," he said. "Guy and girl, taking refuge against the storm, swept away by the power of their feelings . . ."

The closer he got, the more Joey felt her resistance wearing down, the wall of fear—if that's what it was—crumbling. She felt herself leaning in to him, turning her face up to his face . . .

And then she pulled back. Wait a minute. This wasn't a movie. It wasn't some guy and girl up on the screen who'd gotten lost in the storm. This wasn't the perfect movie moment. This was real life.

Dawson continued to look into Joey's eyes, to explore her face with his gaze. She could almost feel his glance, as if it were a caress. A wave of giddy dizziness washed over her. On the other hand, what was wrong with being swept away by your feelings?

"So I've been doing all the sharing so far," Steve said lightly. He got up and put another log on the fire, his arm muscles lean but strong. Jen watched him coax the fire back to life. Definite babe material, in his old paint-splattered jeans, and black T-shirt. He replaced the fireplace grate and sat back down next to her on the sofa. "Now it's your turn. Tell me about you."

Jen laughed. "Deal's a deal. Let's see. Born and raised in New York City—until now. Living with my grandmother in Capeside since the beginning of school this year. Favorite color, pale blue. Favorite old movie, *A Streetcar Named Desire.* Favorite sport, riding. I won a blue medal at the junior regionals. Best subject, History. Worst subject, Algebra."

"So . . . why did *you* leave the big city, Jen?" Steve asked.

Jen felt uncomfortable. The big question. The one she'd avoided with Dawson for way too long. Or maybe not long enough. "Well . . . same reason as you, it sounds like. I needed to slow down, too," she answered, her words marked by hesitation.

Steve didn't push for details. He simply nodded and accepted what she'd said. "Welcome to the club." There was an easy understanding behind his words.

Jen relaxed into a smile. Steve flashed the lopsided grin. "Boyfriend?" he asked, going on to the next question.

"You're asking all the hard ones," Jen said teasingly. "No. No one right now," she answered. But she couldn't keep Dawson from popping into her head.

She'd broken up with Dawson to be on her own. At least that's what she'd told him. To sort out her confusion of feelings. To figure out who she really was, without a guy to lean on. She wasn't sure she was any closer to the answer. Yet here she was, feeling a powerful growing attraction to Steve, and hoping his dryer would never, ever stop going around.

Still, she'd made it clear to Dawson that she was ready to try again with him. And he'd had different ideas, which didn't include her. So if she found herself falling for someone else's smile, it wasn't anyone's business but her own.

A bolt of lightning split the sky outside Steve's living room window. She hoped that Dawson wasn't still out in that storm, that he and Joey weren't wet and cold and frightened somewhere.

She finished the last sip of her hot chocolate. "Refill?" Steve asked.

"Sure," Jen said.

"Don't go anywhere," he joked.

"You're holding my clothes hostage," Jen reminded him.

"Oh, yeah. That. Funny how it's taking such a long time for them to dry," Steve said with a grin.

Jen grinned back. "Funny."

"I'd say they need about another couple of weeks."

Jen laughed as Steve disappeared into the kitchen. Wherever everyone else was, she was where she wanted to be.

Pacey would rather have been just about anywhere else. He lay back on his cot and squeezed his eyes shut. It was the only way he could avoid looking at Sylvie. But he knew she was there, right across the room, and he knew she was as aware of him as he was of her. Aware and hurting and angry.

Around him, it sounded like a party—people talking and laughing. Someone had gotten ahold of a radio, and vintage Doors were singing about Riders on the Storm. The sounds of a basketball game competed with the radio—the uneven rhythm of the basketball on the floor, the squeak of sports shoes that were still damp, the clatter of the ball meeting the backboard.

"Yo, Witter, heads up!"

Pacey's eyes flew open just as some mystery object came whizzing by his head. He followed its trajectory. It fell to the floor nearby, a gelatinous amoeba of chocolate pudding.

Pacey got to his feet. Stupid Times at Ridgemont High. He couldn't help glancing over toward Sylvie. She was studiously avoiding him, offering him a view of her back.

Pacey shifted uncomfortably from one bare foot to the other and back. He didn't much feel like calling winners of the one-on-one game of hoops—even though he could have beaten Keith Silves and Beau Williams shooting lefty. And given his mood, the music sounded funereal. Hadn't those guys heard that Jim Morrison was way dead? As far as the talking and joking, it only made him more aware of how bleak he felt by comparison. And he knew Sylvie wished he'd vanish off the face of the earth. Or at least the gym.

Pacey felt a tightness in his chest and throat. He shoved his feet into his damp basketball sneakers. He didn't know where he was going, but he needed to go. To get some air, to take a walk, to run away from the way he was feeling.

The first blast of wind and rain actually felt good in a twisted, pain-is-pleasure sort of way. Stung his face. Burned his lungs as he breathed it in. He steeled his body for the onslaught and started walking. A dark, wet road curved away from the school. At the first fork, he went left. He had to lean into the wind as he walked. The tree branches gesticulated frantically.

But as he focused on his battle with the elements, Pacey's head began to clear. He kept walking and walking, past a few houses lit from inside, and many more that were dark. Not a single car passed on the road. Pacey was every bit as soaked as he'd been before they were rescued. His short plaid pants clung to his legs like plastic wrap.

He kept moving, leaving Sylvie behind, leaving behind the unhappiness he'd caused her. A bolt of lightning split the sky. For a shimmering moment, Pacey could see the ocean up ahead and to his left. It gave him something to focus on. A goal. He walked more quickly. Another streak of lightning illuminated the narrower road that led toward the beach. He could hear the huge waves crashing against the shore.

He didn't stop until he was standing at the summit of a massive sand dune. It dropped off sharply just in front of him. The tide was so high that the ocean came right up to the base of the dune. A wave rolled in like a bulldozer and crashed into the mountain of sand. A mix of cold salt spray and sand stung Pacey's face. He could barely see.

But he didn't budge. Maybe he could walk off the guilt he felt, drive out the memory of Sylvie's hurt, drive out the realization of how much she must despise him. And he deserved every bitter drop of her hate.

Chapter 13

Joey was so close. Dawson could feel the sweet warmth of her skin, and smell the floral scent of her shampoo mixing with the freshness of the rain. Her skin was smooth and soft-looking; her eyes were clear and shining with possibility. Her lips were full—and so near. Dawson held his breath. She wasn't pulling back this time. Did he dare make a move? Did she want him to? They were so close that Dawson could feel himself shaking.

"Dawson," Joey whispered, and he could feel her breath as she spoke.

"Yeah?" Shaking, trembling—he couldn't help it.

"Dawson, you're shivering," Joey said softly. "Look, why don't you . . ." Her words trailed off as she unzipped the jacket he'd given her and held it open in invitation. "Maybe there's enough room for both of us," she said.

Dawson felt a rush of euphoria. This moment wasn't going to get away. He slid closer and let Joey wrap the jacket around both of them. It felt absolutely natural to slip his arms around her waist as she enveloped them in warmth.

He let himself enjoy the feel of their bodies pressed together, her cheek against his cheek, their arms entwined.

"I can see it now," Joey whispered. "The two people from long ago, whoever they were, in front of a roaring fire in their warm little house, safe from the world. . . ."

Dawson breathed in deeply, breathed in Joey's nearness. He was warming up. He felt his tension melting away. The trembling subsided. "Safe from the world," he echoed softly. He pulled back just enough to look at her face again. To look into her brown eyes.

"What?" Joey whispered.

"Nothing. You . . . look so pretty," Dawson answered honestly. Joey really didn't know how beautiful she was.

"I do?"

He nodded and gently held his palm to her cheek. Warm bare skin on warm bare skin, erasing the cold, erasing the dampness. No more talking. No more thinking, even. Pacey was right. Whatever you do, do it. Don't just think about it. Don't just talk about it.

And then all thoughts of Pacey disappeared into the night. All thoughts of anything. And there was only this feeling, this yearning, and nothing was going to get in the way this time.

Dawson and Joey drew together. . . .

Jen and Steve had finished their hot chocolate. The fire had burned down to an orange glow. The dryer had stopped. But neither one of them made any move to get up.

"So, Jen, are you happy in Capeside?" Steve asked, draping one arm over the back of the sofa. "What about you? Would you think of moving back to New York?"

Another toughie. "You make a girl think, Steve."

"Yeah? Is that a good thing?" Steve followed one question with another.

Jen laughed. "Sure. It's always a good sign when a guy's interested in a girl's brain. I'm just not sure I have an answer to that question. New York . . . It can be the most exciting city in the whole world. All the different people from different places. The energy. Not to mention all the clubs and restaurants and theaters and everything."

In her mind's eye, Jen could see herself hanging out up on the Hill in Central Park on a sunny day, watching the procession of people—runners and in-line skaters of every age, size, and shape, the orange and green spiked-haired dad pushing an angel-faced baby in a stroller, the dreadlocked skater dancing to the beat of music only he could hear on his Walkman, the guy with the long gray hair who always wore purple and rode around on a purple bike, tots on tricycles, bikini-clad sunbathers. . . .

And after a day in the park, a night out. Maybe

some Jamaican food at that little place downtown with the four-alarm jerk chicken and the homemade ginger beer. Then maybe a night of dancing at a new club, or some party-hopping with a group of friends.

"Yeah, I miss it," Jen told Steve. "There isn't anyplace in the world like it. And it's my hometown, you know? That makes me miss it even more. But I don't know . . . Capeside has it charms, too." Jen pictured herself walking down Main Street on a sunny afternoon. "People say hi to me on the street in town. The tellers at the bank know me. The people who work at the supermarket, they ask me about my day. Maybe that kind of thing sounds silly, but I like it."

Steve laughed. "Yeah, I remember this one time the woman at the little grocery store here was bagging my stuff for me, and she commented on how I'd forgotten to buy my usual box of double-fudge cookies."

"Well, that might be a little *too* small-town for me," Jen said. "But still, there's something about people knowing you that makes you feel like it's your town. Even if you haven't been there that long. And then it definitely beats New York in the natural-beauty category. The beaches, the water—it just somehow makes me feel better, no matter what. I mean, if I'm feeling lousy about something, I go take a walk by the water and it practically always helps."

"Negative ions," Steve said. "At least that's what they tell me. The ocean's loaded with 'em. Good for the spirit."

"Whatever." Jen laughed. "Maybe it's just being able to take a walk someplace pretty whenever I want. Just out the front door and go, even at night. That's one of the things I like most—being able to walk by myself at night."

"Not a specialty of New York," Steve commented.

"Not exactly. The thing is, it's like you said earlier. You make your own sense of belonging. Or not." Jen felt the corners of her mouth tug down. Her body tightened. "I think . . . you have to be at peace with yourself to feel at home anywhere."

"And you aren't there yet," Steve said quietly.

Jen swallowed hard. "I don't know. I guess . . . not. I think I had this idea that it would be as easy as moving to a new place. Or at least that's what my father seemed to think when he sent me to Capeside. But the past really kind of follows you, doesn't it? Or you carry it with you."

"I understand, Jen. I really do," Steve said. "But it gets easier. I personally promise. As you get a little older, you learn how to put some of those demons from the past to rest. And, well, I hope that doesn't sound condescending or patronizing or like I think I'm some wise old man."

Too handsome for a wise old man. But it did remind Jen, just for a moment, that Steve was Mr. Yarrow, teacher, a grown-up, even if he was a total babe. "No, that's okay," she said. "In fact, it's nice to hear. Nice that it gets a little easier as you go along."

"Living all by yourself for a while will do it," Steve said. "At least it did for me. Spent a lot of time by myself—for the first time, really. Had to really face myself, take a good look at myself, figure out what I liked about who I was and what I didn't, and where I wanted to go. Inside my head, I mean. Does that sound incredibly flaky?"

Jen shook her head. "It makes perfect sense. But it sounds like awfully hard work."

"It can be." Steve grinned the lopsided grin. And Mr. Yarrow was gone and Steve was back.

Jen sighed. "Do you ever wish you could just sail away from everything? Disappear to some faraway place where no one knows you and you can just invent yourself from scratch?"

"There are some faraway places I definitely wouldn't mind seeing," Steve said easily. "It's up there on my wish list. To go around the globe one day. Hit all five continents. Pack light. One pair of really comfortable walking shoes."

"Sounds wonderful." Jen let herself sink even deeper into the sofa cushions. "Steve, you know that story about that ship that sank out here in the colonial times? And the pirate and his wife?"

"The *Whydah,*" Steve said. "And Black Sam Bellamy and Goody Hallett."

"Goody? I thought she was Maria."

"Goody was what they called all the women back then. Goodwife. Like Mrs. Maria Hallett. But you got the wife version. I know the one where she's his girlfriend." Steve laughed. "You got the PG version. Mine's NC-17."

"Oh, then, you missed the secret wedding in the apple orchard," Jen told him. "That part was good. The whole story was good."

"Yeah, we're pretty proud of our local legend, around here," Steve said lightly. "But what about Sam and Maria?"

Jen sighed. "Well, what if Sam didn't really drown? What if he just let people believe he had? Because it was convenient. Because he needed to evade capture as a notorious pirate. Because his wife—or girlfriend—had been banished from her community. They were outcasts. Outlaws. But they were in love. They had each other. And their little baby."

"I think I like this version," Steve said. "Very romantic." He leaned toward her. "Go on, Jen. Let's hear the rest of it."

Jen was intensely aware of Steve's nearness. "Well, what if they sailed off where nothing could catch up with them?" she whispered. "Where no one cared where they'd been or what they'd done." She looked into Steve's chocolate-brown eyes. "Maybe they sailed off to some desert island, or traveled around the world."

"With one pair of shoes apiece," Steve added softly, smiling. "It sounds like an adventure—with the right person."

Jen could see tiny flecks of gold in Steve's eyes. They held each other's gaze wordlessly. Jen felt heady, dizzy. Who was this guy who seemed to share her very thoughts and emotions? Whom she barely knew but felt so close to? Who was so heart-stoppingly handsome that she was almost ready to give up everything but a single measly pair of shoes and hop the next freighter to travel the world with?

Jen and Steve drew together. . . .

Pacey could have sworn he saw a shadowy figure walking in the dunes. He squeezed his eyes shut.

They had to be playing tricks on him. It had to be the sting of the rain and wind and the saltwater spray of the angry ocean. Night was approaching. He was by himself on the edge of land, in a strange place. It was just too easy to invent things in a situation like this. There wasn't any ghost out there on the dunes. He had to be imagining it.

But when he opened his eyes, she was still there. Barely visible through the rain and fog but not invisible enough to ignore. A woman's figure. Alone. Walking the dunes. Pacey felt a jolt of fear. No sane, living, breathing woman would be out here walking around on a night like this. The sky was quickly growing dark. Yet she kept walking. Pacey's pulse beat in this throat. Oh, my God, she was coming closer! The shadowy phantom was getting bigger.

He turned away from her. No. He wouldn't let himself believe it. Maria Hallett was not coming after him on the dunes. He walked hurriedly in the opposite direction. It wasn't happening. If he ignored her, she would go away. What could a nearly three-hundred-year-old ghost want with him, anyway?

"Boo!" said a throaty voice behind him.

Pacey let out a startled cry as he whirled around. His terror turned instantly to pure humiliation. "Sylvie!"

Sylvie studied him carefully. "Well, who did you think it was? Maria Hallett?"

Pacey was glad it was dark and stormy. Otherwise Sylvie would have seen his face go from pale as a—well, a ghost—to pink to burning, shameful bright red.

But Sylvie didn't seem to need the color cues. "You did!" she exclaimed, her eyes widening. "Pacey, you thought I was Maria Hallett!" She let out a peal of laughter that seemed completely incongruous with the bad weather.

Pacey gave an embarrassed shrug. "It's not exactly living-people weather out here tonight."

Sylvie laughed even harder. "A ghost! You admit it! Oh, my God, if I wanted to get even with you, I'd go right back to the school and blast this news all over the gym."

Pacey felt a gust of apprehension. "Is that what you want? To get even with me?"

Sylvie shook her head. She was still giggling.

"Oh. Well, good. I mean, at least I made you laugh."

Sylvie wiped her eyes. "You sure did." Her laughter began to subside. "You should have seen your expression, Pacey."

"Look, it *is* sort of a raw night to be out for a little walk by the water," Pacey tried to defend himself. "What are you doing out here, anyway?"

"Looking for you," Sylvie said. Her voice softened. "Why are *you* out here, Pacey? Didn't you get enough of the weather on Billings Island today?"

Pacey sighed. "Punishment, maybe. I guess I felt like I deserved it. That and I figured you didn't want me anywhere around you."

"Maybe I didn't. But I didn't mean to drive you out here with the ghosts." Sylvie gave a little smile.

It was like a light in the storm. Her eyes shone with a compassion that Pacey didn't quite feel he deserved. Her face wet with rain, she looked radiant . . . lovely, even. Warmed by her smile, by her ability to forgive, Pacey suddenly couldn't understand how he hadn't seen her inner beauty right away.

And it made him feel even more like a loser for the way he'd made her feel. "If I could take back what I said, I would," he said softly.

She nodded. "I know. I shouldn't have been so tough on you back there. I know it must have been hard to be so brutally honest with me about how you feel."

"Brutal. You got that much right," Pacey said regretfully.

"Look, Pacey. I wish you could take it back, too. At least as much as you do, believe me. It hurts that I'm not as pretty as, well, Jen, for instance, and a lot of other girls. And it hurts that looks do count, no matter what they tell you. But I know they do. And I guess it's just a fantasy that you could look at me and think I looked like Jennifer Love Hewitt. About as likely as meeting a ghost."

Pacey's embarrassment returned full force. "Add gullible coward to my list of qualities."

Sylvie shook her head. "No. I don't mean to make fun of you, any more than you meant to make fun of me. I guess I'm still really hurt, but I don't want you walking around in the freezing rain all night, Pacey. I don't want you catching pneumonia on my account, or it'll be my fault when your spirit winds up walking the cliffs with our ghost friend," she said teasingly. And then she added more somberly, "Poor girl."

Sylvie turned to look out at the ocean. Pacey followed her gaze. The rough water sparkled with phosphorescence, tiny pinpoints of light stirred up by the wild currents and the pounding elements. The swells rolling in appeared to be lit up.

"Imagine coming out here day after day, night after night," Sylvie said softly, "Looking out at this vastness, praying for a ship on the horizon. It's so huge. It can make you feel so small, so insignificant, so alone. And Maria grew old just looking out to sea like this, knowing the one she was waiting for would never come home. Knowing no one would ever love her. No one there for her as the years went on. No one to hold her, no one to share her life with. . . ."

Pacey realized that Sylvie was crying, tears flowing down her cheeks and mixing with the rain. He took a step nearer to her and put his hand on her arm. "Sylvie . . . it's a story. A myth. A legend. Maybe Maria Hallett met someone new, after Sam's ship went down. People do. She could have married again."

"Maybe. If she was as beautiful as the legends say." Sylvie's voice was still shaking. A wave crashed below them. "But maybe she just got old alone."

Pacey felt a fresh spray of guilt. "Sylvie, Maria's fate isn't going to be your fate. Don't think it for a second. Not someone like you. Not someone as smart and funny and—" Suddenly words weren't enough. And suddenly he just found himself putting his arms around Sylvie, gently, tenderly pulling her toward him.

"Pacey, what are you doing?" she whispered.

"Just take the moment," he begged her. "Only the moment. You're not a lonely ghost, Sylvie. You're a vivacious young woman who knows how to savor life." And as he said it, he felt the truth of his words; he felt his attraction overpower his hesitation. He felt how right it was to have Sylvie in his arms.

Pacey and Sylvie drew together.

Chapter 14

Joey savored the moment before the kiss. She and Dawson, their lips almost touching. She was acutely aware of everything around her—the wind whistling through the trees, the rain on the leaky roof, the roll of thunder somewhere in the distance.

Yet at the same time there was nothing but the two of them. The feel of his heart beating against her body, his scent mingling with the sharp freshness of the storm. She was almost falling into his gaze, his soul. His mouth was so close to her mouth, she could feel the electricity.

Lightning split the sky, and when the thunder echoed through the night, their lips met. A moment of tender uncertainty. Mouths gentle, soft, a shared breath. A sweet, delicate kiss, and then a more passionate one. More hunger. Mouth against mouth with more pressure, more urgency. Hot, moist, drinking each other in, exploring, tasting . . .

Joey let out a soft moan. They pressed together. His hands were moving through her hair, stroking her. In the shared warmth of his jacket she felt the lean muscles of his back through his thin T-shirt. Their kisses went even deeper.

But suddenly Joey felt a piercing jolt of fear. She pulled back and looked into Dawson's hazel eyes, again. "What are we doing, Dawson? What does this mean?"

"Joey, maybe you're so lost in the forest you can't see the trees." Dawson's voice was breathless, intense. "If you want to know what it means, then feel it. Don't ask it. This is your answer."

And then he was kissing her again. And she was kissing him back. And time seemed to lose all grasp, and it was only their mouths and their bodies, their hands, their hearts. . . .

And in that fluid moment, Joey really did know the answer. She wrapped her arms around him even more tightly and let herself get lost in their kisses.

Pacey savored the moment before the kiss. He and Sylvie, their lips almost touching. He was acutely aware of everything around him—the wind whipping up the water and sand, the rain falling on their faces, the roll of thunder reverberating across the ocean.

Yet at the same time there was nothing but the two of them, the feel of her heart beating against his body, her scent mingling with the sharp freshness of the storm. He was almost falling into her hazel-eyed gaze, her fiery soul. His mouth was so close to her mouth, he could feel the electricity.

Lightning split the sky, and when the thunder echoed through the night, their lips met. A moment of tender uncertainty. Mouths gentle, soft, a shared breath. A sweet, delicate kiss, and then a more passionate one. More hunger. Mouth against mouth with more pressure, more urgency.

Pacey let out a soft moan. They pressed together. His hands were stroking Sylvie's wet, silky hair. She warmed his cold, shivering body by running her hands up and down his back. Their kisses went even deeper.

And then suddenly Sylvie was pulling back. She looked into his eyes again, and he saw a jolt of fear. "What are we doing, Pacey? What does this mean?"

He heard her hesitancy, her fear of getting hurt—again. "Sylvie, let me erase the words I said before," he whispered in her ear. He could barely catch his breath. His lips longed for her lips, again. "Forget what I said. Forget what happened. Forget what you heard. If you want to know how I really feel, then here's your answer. . . ."

Pacey took her wet face between his hands and planted a gentle kiss on Sylvie's forehead. On each of her closed eyes. On the tip of her nose. He brushed her lips with his lips. Her mouth felt so soft. He kissed her mouth again. And then she was kissing him back. The rain streamed down their faces.

Lightning and thunder measured out the pulse of the storm, but for Pacey time seemed to lose all grasp. It was only their mouths and their bodies, their hands and their hearts. . . .

And in that fluid moment, Pacey knew he'd found his mermaid. He wrapped his arms around her even more tightly and let himself get lost in their kisses.

Jen savored the moment before the kiss. She and Steve, their lips almost touching. She was acutely aware of everything around her—the wind whistling through the trees outside, the rain on the high roof, the cozy warmth of the room, the roll of thunder somewhere in the distance.

Yet at the same time there was nothing but the two of them. She was almost falling into his brown-eyed gaze, his soul. His mouth was so close to her mouth, she could feel the electricity.

Or was it the storm? Lightning split the sky. When the thunder echoed through the night, Jen felt herself give a little start. She pulled back in a moment of uncertainty.

Steve sensed it and drew away ever so slightly. "Jen?" he said softly.

"What are we doing, Steve? What am I doing?"

Steve shook his head gently. "Am I going too fast for you?"

Jen sighed and leaned back on the sofa. She'd had her moment—her moment with Steve where time had started to lose its grasp, where his lips were so near all she had to do was lean forward a whisper, a breath, and he would have been kissing her and she would have been drinking him in . . .

But just the other night she'd thought it was Dawson she wanted, Dawson's kisses, Dawson's embrace that would make time melt away. How could she go from one guy to another so quickly and effortlessly? Wanting each of them so much that for a fluid moment each had seemed like the only guy in the world?

Jen's head reeled. She felt out of breath. More lightning and thunder, marking the storm. Dawson—was he still out there in the cold, dark night? Were he and Joey lost in the storm while she was in here, falling into Steve's arms?

Jen let her eyes close for a moment. Well, not kissing Steve wasn't going to help Dawson if he was still out there. But kissing him wasn't going to change anything either, was it? When tomorrow came, nothing would be any different. Steve here alone in his little house. Jen in Capeside, a raw bundle of mixed emotions.

She opened her eyes and looked at Steve, again. So handsome, she almost couldn't resist. So much the kind of guy she could see herself falling madly, truly, deeply in love with. But it wasn't their time or place. Not here. Not now. Not when Jen was trying so hard to make sense of all her tumultuous emotions.

"It's okay, Jen," Steve said softly. He seemed to understand.

"I'm just . . . so tired all of a sudden," Jen told him, and as she said it, she realized it was true. She'd probably walked nearly twenty miles today in the wind and rain and biting weather. Was it really only this morning that she'd been up on the deck of the *Princessa,* jumping up and down with Dawson at the sight of the whales swimming right up alongside the boat? It seemed more like a week ago. So much had happened.

"Listen, why don't you take a little nap?" Steve

suggested. "It's probably a lot quieter than it's going to be over at the gym. I'll get you over there before anyone goes anywhere. If that doesn't make you feel uncomfortable, I mean."

Jen smiled. This guy had to be a 10 on the nice-meter as well as the cute-meter. "I'm about as comfortable as I've been in a long, long time, Steve. The truth is, I'm so comfortable I don't really want to leave at all. Ever." She gave a self-conscious litte laugh. "But I am going to leave, and this is going to be over. We're going to be over. So it's better that we don't start. . . . Am I making any sense at all?"

"I think I'm following. I guess I'd rather be following a different train of thought, but I do understand, Jen."

"Thanks. Thanks, Steve. And that nap? It sounds wonderful."

A few minutes later Jen was stretched out on the sofa. Steve was spreading a down quilt over her. She felt deliciously sleepy. "Sweet dreams, Jen," Steve said. He planted a soft, chaste kiss on her forehead.

Jen had a powerful urge to wrap her arms around him and pull him toward her and forget everything she'd told him, everything she'd told herself.

But the moment passed, and he stepped away. She let out a long, slow breath. Was she being sensible and mature, or was she just missing out? She let her heavy eyelids close. She snuggled under the blanket. She wrapped her arms around herself. Maybe, if she was lucky, she'd dream about kissing him.

Chapter 15

"Quick, Pacey! We're leaving puddles!" Sylvie egged him on, in between fits of giggles. They stood in the hall of the school, outside the gym, peering in through the little window in the top part of the door.

"I have to put myself in the moo-o-o-d," Pacey said dramatically, his words also punctuated by laughter. "Get myself into the part, live the emotions . . . Any Acting 101 coach will tell you that."

"We're not making a movie here, Pacey. You just have to create a distraction so I can snag that bag of clothes. I really don't want to start explaining to everyone why you and I didn't think we got wet enough the first time out—especially not to my dad. Besides, that woman already told us—one outfit to a customer."

Pacey looked into the gym. The woman with the white braid was still sitting at the long table on which they'd spread out the food and beverages, even though the Capeside crowd had done a serious number on the eats, and only some messy-looking leftovers remained. The huge black plastic trash bag full of old clothes was under the table. "She's over there guarding the table like she's got a bag of jewels hidden under there," Pacey said.

"She'll be the first one up when you run in there. I can tell just by looking at her, Pacey. If anyone believes the legend, she does."

Pacey shook his head. "I don't know how you talked me into this. I'm going to be the laughing-stock of the school when it's over."

"Pacey, I thought you told me you already were the laughingstock of the school."

"Oh. Yeah, well, this will certainly clinch my reputation." Pacey took a deep breath. "Are you ready?"

Sylvie nodded.

"Okay, then. One . . . two . . . three!" Pacey pushed open the door and burst into the gym. "Ghost!" he shouted at the top of his lungs. He did his best to look scared. Actually it wasn't that hard. He just re-created the moment when he'd been sure Maria Hallett was walking toward him on the dunes.

He felt all eyes in the room turning toward him. He took several frantic-looking steps to one side, drawing the fire. He waved his hands over his head in an exaggerated gesture. "Maria Hallett! I saw her! I swear it!" Out of the corner of his eye, Pacey saw

Sylvie dash into the gym and make a crouched beeline for the food table.

"Witter, give it a rest!" someone yelled out. It sounded like Cliff Elliot.

"No, really!" Pacey insisted loudly. "Look! Right up there above the basketball hoop! She's hovering. Don't you see her?"

"I think his brain got waterlogged," someone else yelled out.

"Don't forget that's the same guy who entered the Miss Windjammer pageant. He's definitely got a bunch of screws loose."

Maybe, thought Pacey, *but at least I've got your attention.* And Sylvie was right. The woman with the braid was on her feet. She and everybody else stared at him, following his wild gestures toward the basketball net at the far end of the gym. Meanwhile Sylvie had grabbed the huge plastic garbage bag and was beating an exit.

Pacey waited until she pushed open the gym door. "Over there!" he shouted. He traced an imaginary arc with his finger, from the basketball hoop to the door to the girls' locker room. "She's heading for the locker room. Check her out!"

Heads swiveled toward the girls' locker room, despite the utter skepticism in the gym. Eyes off him for a moment, Pacey bolted at top speed. He crashed out the door and into the hall, on Sylvie's heels. "Hurry! This way," he shouted, grabbing the bag from her and taking off down the corridor. They sprinted around a corner and into the stairwell, trailing watery footprints and uncontrollable laughter.

They didn't stop until they found themselves up on the top floor by a long bank of lockers. Pacey put the bag of loot down and collapsed on the tile floor, trying to catch his breath through bursts of giggling.

Sylvie crashed down next to him. "Hovering over the basketball hoop?" she whooped. "Heading toward the girls' locker room? What, Maria Hallett's been waiting three hundred years to use the little girls' room?"

They both cracked up. "Well, it worked, didn't it?" Pacey asked, patting the big plastic bag.

"Yeah. Let's take a look at the treasure, Cap'n Sam," Sylvie said. She opened up the bag and started rummaging around in it. "Not exactly rubies and gold," she mused. "Jeez, can you believe somebody actually designed this thing?" She held up a shapeless housecoat of a dress in an offensive pink-and-army-green-striped fabric.

"I guess we didn't get the bag with the Versaces and the Calvin Kleins," Pacey said.

Sylvie raised an eyebrow. "Not exactly. Oh, but look! This is just perfect!" With a triumphant flourish, she pulled a beige terry-cloth bathrobe out of the bag and started using it to dry off her face and hair. When she'd finished, she handed it to Pacey, and he did the same.

He felt Sylvie studying him as he toweled off. "So . . . is it true that you entered a girls' beauty pageant, Pacey?"

Pacey felt a rush of embarrassment. "Well . . . yeah. But to make a point. I mean, it's discrimination, that girls-only business. Why should they be the only ones to qualify for that nice cash prize?"

"Uh-huh. Okay, Pacey." Sylvie raised an eyebrow at him. Then she went back to sifting through the clothes. "Well, so maybe this lovely skirt would be an appropriate change of clothes for you, then." Sylvie pulled a swath of brassy metallic fabric out of the bag, unfurling it to reveal a long—and totally tasteless—skirt, replete with fake gold buttons and fake gold trim, and a spray of glittery plastic sequins down the front.

"Watch out!" Pacey said, dramatically covering his eyes with the back of his hand. "You could blind a guy with that thing, you know." He peeked through the space between his fingers for a better look. "On second thought . . ." Pacey felt an impish smile steal over his face. He uncovered his eyes. "It's perfect!"

Sylvie shot him a long look. "It is? You really are into this beauty queen thing, aren't you? Emphasis on the word . . . Well, never mind."

"Oh, not for me," Pacey said hurriedly. "I've gotten more than enough attention already tonight. Actually I was thinking about that lovely skirt for you, Sylvie."

"No way." Sylvie shoved the gold confection back into the plastic bag.

"Aw, come on. Humor me," Pacey said. "Look, I have another confession to make, Sylvie."

"Oh?"

"I . . . um, well, I've kind of got this idea in my head that you're a lovely mermaid, come out of the depths to make my fantasies real. And if you kind of squint and look at that skirt thing in a certain way, you have to admit, it *is* the perfect mermaid costume."

Sylvie arched an eyebrow. "You *do* have some screws loose, Pacey." Then she softened. "But, hey, I doubt anyone's thought of me as a lovely mermaid before."

"So you'll wear it?"

Sylvie bit her lip.

"Come on," Pacey encouraged. "Then I can look across the room—across that sea of cots, if you will—and see my mermaid woman."

"I don't know, Pacey. The whole idea of this was to be a little discreet."

"And gold sequins isn't discreet?"

"I just don't relish having to tell my dad I followed some strange guy out onto the dunes in the storm. And I do mean strange." Sylvie laughed.

"So you'll just deny you were wearing anything different when you left the gym. That's what I'm going to do. 'What are you talking about, Dad?' " Pacey mimicked. " 'How could you possibly have missed this thing the first time around?' He'll think *he's* the one who's going nuts. Come on, live dangerously, Sylvie."

Sylvie considered it for a few moments. She took the gold skirt back out and studied it as if it were a disease. Then she looked at Pacey and started laughing. "Okay, Pacey. I may not be as weird as you, but, hey, if we can't have a little fun in this situation, what's the point? But on one condition."

"What's that?" Pacey asked.

"That *I* get to pick out *your* outfit, too."

"Had to be a catch," Pacey said. "On the other hand, how much worse could it be than these?" He tugged at the now-drenched plaid pants. "Or that skirt? All right, then. You're on."

Sylvie went right to work. Clothes flew from the big bag as she inspected and rejected. A few minutes later she presented Pacey with the outfit she'd pulled together.

Pacey held the pieces up one by one. Plain black pants. Okay, so far so good. Maybe a little big, but nothing too awful. A white shirt. Fine. Wait a minute. What were all these frilly flourishes down the front of it? "I think you gave me a woman's shirt," he told Sylvie.

"Tuxedo shirt. Too froufrou for my taste, too, but just what I'm looking for, right now. Nope—no complaints. You want me in the gold thing, you're putting that on."

Pacey grimaced as he ran a finger down the ruffle. Yuck. But still not as cheesy as the gold skirt, he had to admit. He gave in with a little nod.

"And then this. And this." Sylvie handed him the final two pieces—a dark vest and a red bandana. "Wrap the bandana around your head," she instructed.

"Hippie in a tuxedo?" Pacey asked, confused. And then he put the whole outfit together in his mind's eye and he suddenly got it. "A pirate! I'll look like a pirate! Like—"

"Captain Sam Bellamy," Sylvie finished, delighted. "You have your little fantasy and I have mine."

Pacey grinned. "Okay, the pirate and the mermaid. Yeah, that makes sense, I suppose. What self-respecting pirate would come home to some pilgrim woman in drab black and white, when he could have a mermaid in gold lamé?"

"Yup. So now you know the secret about why Captain Sam never made it home to Maria." Sylvie laughed.

A few minutes later Pacey was in his "dressing room" behind one end of the bank of lockers, while Sylvie was in her "dressing room" down at the other end. His wet clothes in a pile next to him, Pacey pulled on his new outfit, buttoning and zipping, and tucking his hair under the bandana.

"Don't forget to tie a knot in each pant leg, around the bottom," Sylvie called out to him. "So they balloon out and then come back in tight at the ankle, harem style. That's the finishing touch."

"Aye-aye," Pacey called back. He followed her orders and stepped out from behind the lockers.

A flash of gaudy gold and Sylvie appeared, too. Her skirt winked and sparkled garishly under the fluorescent lights of the corridor. She'd topped the skirt with a short-sleeved button-down Hawaiian print shirt decorated with palm trees and sailboats.

"Ah, my mermaid," Pacey said, moving toward her.

"Ah, my pirate prince," Sylvie echoed, moving toward him. "You look absolutely . . . ridiculous," she added.

"You too, my lovely fish."

They stood looking at each other, laughing giddily. Pacey felt overwhelmingly, uncharacteristically happy. It was so easy. He reached toward Sylvie and drew her to him. He kissed her softly, and then longer and deeper. "We could just sail away together. The pirate and the mermaid," he murmured.

Sylvie drew back just enough to look into Pacey's face. "That sounds really nice, Pacey." She kissed his cheek tenderly. "Kind of complicates things that I'm supposed to be back at school tomorrow morning. And that my father probably thinks I went to the ladies' room and fell in. I'm working on a line about studying in the library for my upcoming Spanish test. But if we don't get back to the gym soon, he's going to send the Coast Guard after me."

Pacey let out a long breath. "Well, okay. If we have to. Same plan? I create the distraction and you put back the bag?"

Sylvie nodded.

"People are going to think I'm an idiot," Pacey said. "No. Correction. They already do."

"I don't, Pacey. . . ." He and Sylvie came together in one last twelve-cannon, guns firing, all-out major kiss.

"Ready?" Sylvie whispered, her hand on his face.

Pacey nodded. And then they were retracing their route back to the gym, and he was blasting into the big, crowded room. "I am the ghost of Sam Bellamy!" he roared. "I am here to track down my beloved Maria Hallett!"

Everyone stared at him. "What is your problem, Pacey?" Abby said disgustedly. "And didn't you have on a pair of really unattractive plaid pants before?"

"Did I?" Pacey asked, all innocence.

"Just ignore him and he'll go away," someone suggested. Pacey's classmates and teachers went back to their cards and their conversations and whatever they'd been doing. By then Sylvie had shoved the bag back under the table and was strolling casually across the gym.

Pacey returned to his cot. Sylvie returned to hers. And over the deep green ocean of army blankets, the pirate shared a private smile with his mermaid.

Chapter 16

Joey woke up with a start. Where was she? Half inside, half outside, cold floor under her, but the great outdoors right out there in front of her. She rolled over. Dawson! Sleeping on the ground. Suddenly she remembered the boat, the storm, going around in circles. This ruined shack. She sat up. The sky was still dark. The storm had given way to a gentle but steady rain. She and Dawson were still lost.

Still lost—but very much together. She let the fresh memories roll over her. The stories they'd told. The kisses they'd shared. Especially the kisses. And more kisses . . . Joey could still feel his lips on hers.

She gave a contented sigh and leaned over to look at him. In sleep he seemed younger, more serene, more like the Dawson she'd bunked next to every Friday night for most of their childhood, after a movie marathon and an in-depth analysis of everything they'd watched. All talk. All innocence. Joey studied Dawson's handsome face, the strong lines of his jaw, his closed eyes. It wasn't innocent anymore. It wasn't simple.

She felt an uncomfortable rekindling of the hesitation—the fear, Dawson had called it—that she'd felt earlier, before the kisses. What did it all mean? What was going to happen? Joey put a tentative hand on Dawson's arm. He rolled over, half opened one eye, and shut it again.

"Dawson?" Joey whispered. "You awake?"

No answer.

"Dawson?"

"Huh?"

"Um, about before . . ." Joey began, not entirely sure what she really wanted to say.

"Before what?" Dawson asked groggily.

Joey was suddenly aware of how cold it was. She shivered. Before what? Had their kisses been so unmemorable for Dawson? She lay back down, drawing her knees up to her chest and pulling herself into a little ball. "Before . . . nothing," she said quietly. She shut her eyes, but she was wide awake.

An owl hooted nearby. The rain fell on the patchy roof. Joey thought she could hear the ocean in the distance.

"Joey?" Dawson whispered.

"Yeah?"

And suddenly he was gathering her in a warm hug and they were turning toward each other, and they paused only for a split second before joining in an all-out major kiss. And another. And another . . .

* * *

Jen woke up slowly, stretching deliciously, aware only of how warm and comfortable she was. She half opened one eye. It took her a moment to remember where she was. The field trip, the long walk for help, Steve and his cozy little house.

Jen yawned and opened the other eye too. The sky outside Steve's living room window was the pale blue-gray of predawn. The rain had stopped. A bird let out a single high, sweet note. Jen could smell freshly brewed coffee wafting in from the next room.

"Good morning," Steve said. "Well, almost morning."

Jen sat up. Steve was nearby, perched on a hard-backed chair, a sketchbook open on his lap, a charcoal pencil in his hand. "Hi," Jen said. She remembered the kisses that hadn't happened. She felt a stab of regret.

"Hi. I used you as a model. I hope you don't mind." Steve tapped his sketchbook with his pencil.

Jen felt her cheeks color. "You did? When I was sleeping?"

"I know I should have asked you, but then I would have had to wake you up," Steve said apologetically. "And you looked so comfortable and happy and—asleep."

"Snoring?" Jen asked with a little grimace.

Steve laughed. "Is that what you're worried about? Not a chance. You looked incredibly lovely and peaceful. That's why I couldn't resist."

Jen swung her legs off the couch and got up. "Well, how'd it turn out?" The sweats she'd borrowed from him were warm with sleep as she padded across the polished wood floor in her bare feet.

Steve smiled and gave a little shrug. "You'll have to be the judge." He showed her the sketchbook. "*Sleeping Beauty Number Three.* It took me two other tries before I did you justice. You just looked so . . . serene. I had to get the lines fluid and soft enough."

Jen blinked and rubbed the sleep from her eyes. She studied the picture Steve had made. It was beautiful. She was beautiful, at least through Steve's eyes.

"Like it?" he asked.

Jen nodded. "More than like. Steve, you're really good. If I look like that when I'm asleep, I'm never going to wake up again." She gave a happily embarrassed laugh.

"That would be too bad," Steve said lightly. "I kind of like you when you're awake, too."

Jen was seized with an urge to make up for what she'd passed up last night. It wasn't too late. Or was it?

Steve closed his sketchbook. "Well, I guess we better get you over to the school one of these years," he said, with a note of reticence. "It's not gonna look so good if they have to come knocking on my door to find you."

"I guess," Jen said, just as reticently.

"But listen, if you want, we might be able to catch the sunrise over the ocean first, if we hurry. The sky looks clear. It should be pretty awesome."

Jen felt her spirits pick up. "That sounds really nice."

"So . . . I guess we should see about those clothes that took such a very long time to dry," Steve said.

Jen laughed. "Maybe you need to put a call in to your repairman. Find out what the problem is."

"Uh-huh. Funny how it only acts up when I have certain choice visitors."

A few minutes later Jen had traded in Steve's sweats for her own white jeans and T-shirt and sweater. The sky was getting lighter. "Ready?" Steve asked.

Jen sighed. "I guess . . ." She hiked her knapsack onto one shoulder.

"Coffee for the road? I just made a pot."

"Absolutely. It smells great. A big mug required to wake up properly, to tell you the truth."

"Milk and sugar?"

"Straight up."

"Nothing in it? That's serious," Steve said kiddingly. "But I like a gal who can handle her coffee at full strength."

"And I like a guy who can brew it full strength. Fabulous artist *and* he makes a mean cup of Joe."

Jen and Steve smiled at each other flirtatiously. "Well . . . you know where to find me, Jen, if you ever want to." The casualness of his tone didn't disguise the sincerity of his words.

"I won't forget," Jen responded, just as meaningfully.

"Dawson! Joey!"

"Joey! Dawson!"

They awoke to the sound of their names being called. Dawson opened his eyes slowly. Joey was in his arms, nestled spoon-style, her back to his chest. He snuggled even closer, under the shared shelter of his jacket, not ready to give up the powerful feeling of complete contentment and tenderness.

The sky was starting to get lighter, the gray turning to blue, wispy stripes of pink and orange streaking one particular patch of dawn. Dawson had a flash of realization. Those fiery stripes would be east, out over the ocean, where the sun would just about be pushing up above the horizon for the day. Now that they knew which way was east they were no longer lost. Mystery solved. But big whoop.

Definitely a case of too little too late.

"Dawson!" called a voice outside.

"Joey!" yelled another.

Dawson didn't recognize either of the voices. Joey stirred in his arms. She rolled over and looked at him. "I guess they're playing our song," she said quietly.

Dawson cupped her face in one hand. "I guess," he answered reluctantly. Neither of them moved.

"Where were they yesterday evening, when I was dying to get out of this dump?" Joey asked.

Dawson laughed softly. "Looks a little more like home sweet shack this morning, doesn't it?"

Joey laughed, too. She looked especially beautiful when she was happy.

"We could stay really, really quiet and maybe they'll go away," Dawson suggested.

Joey sighed. "Dawson, we spent the entire day yesterday trying to find our way back." But she didn't make the slightest move to respond to the voices outside.

"But I know where we are, now, Joe. Look. East," Dawson said, pointing to the expanding pink-orange streaks in the sky. "We don't need anybody to bail us out. We'll forage for nuts and berries. Catch fish. Learn to rub two sticks together," he joked.

Joey smiled. "Nice movie moment."

"Yeah, isn't it?" Dawson agreed.

Joey shrugged off the cover of Dawson's jacket and sat up. "Looks like it's going to be a nice day," she said.

"Joey! Dawson!" The voices were getting louder, closer.

Dawson sat up too, the jacket falling on the dirt floor. "Stay with me here, my pirate princess," he whispered in her ear. "Just you and me in our little hideaway."

Joey giggled. "But first we make a little trip to the nearest Home Depot."

Dawson nodded. "Not a bad idea. Maybe I can stop home and get the VCR and a couple of tapes, too. You know, the three you'd most want to bring if you were stranded on a desert island? Tough to narrow it down, though. Let's see . . ."

"Dawson, there was no electricity in this place last time I checked," Joey reminded him.

"Oh. Right. Power generator?" he suggested.

"That's a few centuries away from rubbing two sticks together." Joey got to her feet.

Dawson did too. His clothes were still damp. A hot shower would really hit the spot. "Okay, so I guess we're heading back to the twentieth century, huh?" he said wistfully.

Joey shrugged. "Dawson, there's a whole world out there," she said with a long sigh.

Dawson looked into her brown eyes. A whole world? No thinking. Well, maybe a little less thinking. Dawson knew he just needed to hold on to the feeling of his night alone with Joey.

"Okay, then. So are you ready to go back to civilization?" he asked, holding her gaze.

Joey hesitated. "I don't know, Dawson. But I know I'm going." She looked away.

Dawson felt a jolt of disappointment, punctuated by irritation with himself. Well, what else had he expected her to say? What else could she say?

Dawson bent down to pick up his jacket. He studied the floor, not quite ready to look up at Joey, again. A shiny pebble nearby caught his eye. He stooped and looked more closely. No, it wasn't a pebble. He picked it up. It was an acorn-size piece of smooth, deep green sea glass, burnished by the sea and sand. He turned it over in his palm.

"What did you find, Dawson?" Joey asked, coming up behind him.

Dawson straightened up. He held his open hand out toward her. The sea glass sparkled like a jewel in his palm. "An emerald," he said. "From Captain Sam's buried treasure."

Joey smiled at him. His irritation faded away. "Go ahead," he said. "It's yours. A souvenir."

"Yeah?" Joey reached out. Their hands met for a moment as she took the treasure.

"Joey? Dawson!"

Dawson turned in the direction of the voices. Through the broken windowpane, he saw a flash among the trees. "They're he-e-e-re," he said. "Hello?" he called out, without complete commitment.

"Hello?" he heard a voice shout back to him.

"This way." Joey added her voice to the chorus.

And then the rescue party was coming toward the love shack—two men in uniform, crashing through the underbrush. Dawson saw Joey slip the sparkling sea glass into her pocket.

Chapter 17

Jen and Steve had a front and center view. They stood at the top of a dune, the ocean shimmering before them. Though the high tide had left a lacy stripe of seaweed along the base of the dunes, the storm-charged water had receded enough to reveal a long cresent of deserted sandy beach below them. The air had the crisp, fresh sting of early morning scrubbed clean by the rain. The waves, still huge in the aftermath of the turbulent weather, rolled in dramatically and crashed in a foamy spray on the shore.

Overhead, the sky was blue, with only a light veil of last night's darkness. Out toward the horizon, the blue was even brighter, and shot through with brilliant bands of red and orange and pink, concentrated over the all-important spot where the sun would make its appearance.

Jen raised her coffee mug to her mouth and inhaled deeply. The rich, strong coffee aroma, mixed with the scent of the salt air was overwhelmingly delicious. Next to her, Steve's face was bathed in the early light. They shared the anticipation, not knowing exactly which second the blazing top of the sun would push up above the horizon.

If there was ever a perfect moment, this was it. Jen wanted to capture it, remember it forever.

The flaming colors deepened. Blinding rays shot up into the sky, etching it with a huge crown. You could feel the power about to explode. "Here goes," Steve whispered excitedly. "What do you think? Three . . . two . . . two and a half," he said, stretching out his words.

A smudge of the brightest fuchsia popped onto the horizon abruptly. Jen let out a little gasp of delight. The smudge swelled into a flattened dome. The dome rose until a perfect disk of pink-red floated just above the water. The sky lightened. It was a new day.

Jen let out a long breath of satisfaction. "That was . . . well, 'incredible' doesn't quite do it justice."

"It's more exciting than watching it set, don't you think?" Steve said. "I mean, don't get me wrong. I love a beautiful sunset. But there's something so awe-inspiring about watching it come up."

Jen took a long sip of coffee. It had gotten lukewarm, but she didn't really mind. "I know what you mean. When you watch the sun set, you know where it's going, when. You see it falling. You know when it's going to disappear. When it comes up, you're waiting for it, but it still somehow feels like this big surprise when it pops up."

"Yeah. That's definitely it," Steve agreed. "That and maybe the fact that I'm not usually up at this time to see it. Makes it that much more of a big deal."

Jen nodded. "I've seen it exactly once before, but I was too . . . tired to appreciate it," she added, skirting the exact partied-out circumstances of her only other sunrise. "So I think I'll call this time the first time, if it's okay with you."

Steve flashed the lopsided smile. "I'm honored to share your first time with you, Jen."

"Likewise, Steve. I couldn't have had a better first experience."

They stood looking at each other, touching only with their gazes and their suggestive words. Should she or shouldn't she? Steve had made the first move last time. Now she knew he was waiting to follow her lead. It would have been the easiest thing in the whole world. But once she started, she was afraid she would never be able to stop.

No, she was going home this morning. And Steve was staying here, where he lived, where he taught high school kids—like her. She let go of his gaze. "It's funny," she said, looking out at the rising sun, again. "Right before it comes up, it looks exactly the way it does just after it sets. I mean, if you took a picture of it and showed it to me, I wouldn't have any idea if it was coming or going." She paused and took a deep breath of sea air. "Speaking of which . . ."

"You're ready to go back to civilization?" Steve asked.

Jen hesitated. "I don't know, Steve, but I'm going."

Steve nodded. "Whenever you're ready . . ."

Pacey awoke from a restless sleep. He'd been dozing on and off all night, unable to stay asleep for very long amid the rustling and snoring and whispering in the gym. He knew instantly where he was—lying on a narrow cot, fully dressed except for his shoes, in a secondhand, cobbled-together pirate costume, surrounded by classmates who thought he was a certifiable nut case.

He grinned to himself. Ah, life could be sweet.

He rolled over and sat up, swinging his legs over the edge of the cot and immediately looking across the gym to find Sylvie. She wasn't in her bed, but he didn't have any trouble spotting her right away. She was over in the grown-ups' camp, discussing something with her father. As she gestured and nodded, making small movements, the gold skirt winked like a tacky star.

Sylvie seemed to feel Pacey's eyes on her. She turned and flashed him a private smile.

"Good morning," he mouthed.

She winked before turning back to her father. Pacey continued to study her. When you got to talk to her, got to listen to her stories, share her jokes, know her animated, adventurous spirit, it added something to Sylvie's features and gave her a glow of . . . inner beauty. A concept Pacey would have scoffed at until he met Sylvie, and written off as some kind of P.C. code word for the "friends-only" type. Ya live and learn, Pacey found himself marveling. He'd had more fun last night than he'd had in a very long time. And he thought Sylvie looked totally cute in her ridiculous skirt.

"Ahoy, Captain. Doing some whale watching?" Pacey heard a nasty voice stage-whisper nearby. He whirled around to see Abby walking by and following his gaze.

Pacey fixed Abby with a direct stare. "Mermaid watching," he told her in no uncertain terms.

Abby shrugged. "You're losing it, Pacey. You know that?"

"Lucky me," Pacey said. And he meant it.

"Attention! Attention, everybody!" Dr. Rand put an end to Pacey and Abby's exchange. He stood on the low bleachers at one end of the gym, waving his arms around. "Hello? People?"

The buzz in the room subsided, though a few of the more talented sleepers in the crowd let out low groans as they were roused from dreamland.

"I have a number of happy announcements," Dr. Rand said loudly. "First of all, Dawson Leery and Joey Potter are fine. They were picked up by the park rangers a little while ago, and they'll meet us back at the boat later this morning."

Cheers went up from the crowd. Pacey felt a surge of relief—and a nagging stab of guilt. He'd been so busy playing pirate-and-mermaid last night that he hadn't really thought about Dawson and Joey. Sometimes ya live and *don't* learn, he scolded himself. But he was happy they were safe. He couldn't help wondering if Dawson had gotten the girl, too.

Dr. Rand was still calling out from the bleachers. "Secondly, your dry clothes are ready. Please use the locker rooms to change, and return the borrowed items you're wearing."

Pacey felt a wave of disappointment. He liked impersonating the ghost of Captain Sam. He glanced over at Sylvie. She looked at him and turned her palms up in a what-can-you-do motion.

"Thirdly, there's a bus waiting outside to take us to the boat. We're moving the boat to the harbor right now, so you won't have to worry about another hike to get to her."

More cheers, possibly louder than the ones that had met the announcement about Dawson and Joey.

"Okay, are all you campers ready to go back to civilization?"

Pacey and Sylvie continued to hold each other's gaze across the room. *Not really*, Pacey thought. But he was going. He tried to memorize the image of Sylvie in her outlandish skirt. Her hazel eyes with their mischievous and intelligent sparkle. Her cloud of fiery red hair. Her round face and clear, lightly freckled skin. Her cheeks pink from the outdoors. The feeling of kissing her soft lips in the pouring rain. He wanted to capture it, remember it forever.

What if they just stayed behind?

Steve pulled into the high school parking lot. "Well, here it is."

Jen looked out the passenger window at the school. Big, yet streamlined, it wore the gray-shingled coat of so many of the older buildings she'd seen on the drive from Steve's house, giving it a comfortable blend of modern and old-fashioned. It seemed right for a small-town oceanside school.

"Thinking about enrolling?" Steve said lightly.

"I hear they have a really good art teacher," Jen teased back.

"And a policy against even looking at your students the wrong way," Steve said, more seriously.

"Right. Of course. The heavy hand of reality," Jen said with a sigh. "Well . . . then, I guess this is good-bye."

"I guess," Steve echoed reluctantly.

But neither one of them moved. They sat looking at each other, in the front seat of Steve's car.

"So . . . thank you for everything, Steve," Jen said softly.

"Thank you, Jen."

"It was a beautiful night."

He nodded. "For me, too."

"I won't forget it," she added. The portrait he'd made of her was tucked safely into her day pack, a souvenir that meant more to her than a chestful of pirate's treasure.

"I won't either."

"Well . . ." Jen leaned over and gave Steve a kiss on the mouth. Not a major romantic kiss, but she let her lips linger a moment longer than purely platonic. "I gotta go," she said. And she couldn't have meant it more. Another second with Steve and she was a goner. She wouldn't be getting back on that boat.

She let herself out of the car and ran toward the school. She didn't look back.

Chapter 18

The school parking lot swarmed with people waiting to board the bus. But across the lot, Sylvie sat in the back of a car-service limo, the door open as she said good-bye to her father. Dr. McCann had arranged for her to go straight to the Boston airport instead of returning on the boat and missing her flight back to school.

Pacey stood waiting until Dr. McCann began walking away. Then he quickly headed over. He leaned down and looked into the car. Sylvie was back in her jeans and red jacket, a big day pack on the seat next to her. "Hey," Pacey said.

"Hey," Sylvie responded.

"Well, I guess you're outta here."

"I guess," Sylvie echoed reluctantly.

"Bye, Sylvie."

"Bye, Pacey."

But Pacey didn't move. He continued to lean into the car, looking at Sylvie as she looked at him. "So . . . thank you for everything, Sylvie," he said softly.

"Thank you, Pacey."

"It was a beautiful night."

She nodded. "For me, too."

"I won't forget it," he added. He opened up his jacket conspiratorially, giving her a view of the red bandana tucked into his inside pocket. "Stolen," he said gleefully. "Better than a pirate's jewels."

Sylvie broke into a big smile. "Pacey? I won't forget either." Sylvie fidgeted her day pack, opening it just enough for Pacey to get a tiny glimpse of metallic fabric. "Better than a pirate's gold!" she said.

Pacey grinned. "I guess this means we're thick as thieves?"

"Hey, Witter!" shouted a voice across the parking lot. "This bus isn't gonna wait all day, dude!"

Pacey glanced behind him. Most of his classmates had boarded the bus already, except for a small group that included Abby and Cliff, who were staring right at him.

Pacey turned his back on them. He leaned even farther into the car and gave Sylvie a kiss on the mouth. Not one of the all-out romantic kisses they'd shared the night before, but he let his lips linger a moment longer than purely platonic.

"Don't be a stranger, Pacey, okay?" she said softly.

"I'll be in touch," Pacey assured her, even though he knew he wasn't being quite as honest as he'd been the night before. Sure, he would write a card or two, but it wouldn't be the same. And sooner or later, he'd get hung up on some other girl. It should have been different, but it wasn't, and Pacey knew it. The heavy hand of reality.

Sylvie knew it, too. Pacey could see it in her eyes. "See ya, Pacey," she whispered in her sexy, throaty voice.

"See ya, Sylvie." And then Pacey turned away from the car and ran toward the bus. He didn't look back.

"Pacey! Pacey!" Jen raced across the school parking lot and intercepted him before he boarded the bus.

"Jen!" Pacey stopped, and she caught up with him. "The hiking heroine returns!" he exclaimed.

"Well, you're in a joking mood. Does that mean they found Dawson and Joey?" Jen asked immediately.

Pacey nodded. "Yeah, an hour or two ago. I think they took them to get dried up someplace. Dr. Rand said they're meeting us at the boat."

Jen felt a huge wave of relief. "Oh, that's great! How are they? Did you get any details?"

A funny expression crossed Pacey's face. "Details? Well, only thirdhand. I heard they were fine. Cold and wet, I suppose, but not too much the worse for wear." He seemed to be considering what to say next. "They managed to find a roof over their heads, was what I heard. Kept them from getting totally rocked by the elements."

A house? "That's good. So does that mean they were able to find their way off Billings Island?"

"Um, I don't think so, Jen." Pacey looked down at his basketball shoes. "I think the place they found was that, um, shack that Sylvie told us about."

Oh. Hel-lo. Jen suddenly understood why Pacey was playing coy. "Of course. The love shack," she said evenly. But she felt a shiver of unchecked envy. Dawson and Joey in the love shack. She couldn't help picturing it as looking a little like Steve's cozy little house, even though common sense told her it was an abandoned hovel. Dawson and Joey, huddled against the storm, together. Dawson and Joey talking into the night. Dawson and Joey, just the two of them . . .

Wait. This was crazy. Jen gave her head a hard shake. Wasn't she just—only minutes ago—thinking she could easily stay in this little town? Didn't she feel as if she might be on the brink of running off and marrying Steve in secret in some apple orchard in the middle of the night, as Sam and Maria had done? And here she was suddenly getting the idea that Joey was the lucky one. Boy, she really was confused.

"Well . . . I guess it's good that Dawson and Joey found some shelter while they were waiting to be rescued," Jen finally said. "I mean, they could have been out in that wind and rain in the middle of the night."

"Out in the wind and rain at night . . ." Pacey nodded slowly. Jen noticed the faraway look on his face."Yeah, they could have been. . . ."

"So I guess they were lucky," Jen continued.

"Yeah. I guess. I mean, some people have all the luck. Who wouldn't want to spend a stormy night in some little love shack?"

"Yeah, who wouldn't?" Jen echoed, her thoughts drifting to Steve's safe, bright, warm house. Would she rather have been stranded with Dawson in a cold shack? No. Not really. That wasn't it.

"So you never made it to the Capeside slumber party in the gym, with the rest of us," Pacey commented, almost as if he could read what she was thinking.

"No, I didn't." The gold flecks in Steve's brown eyes, the hot chocolate in front of the fire, the easy conversation, the intelligence behind that irresistible lopsided grin . . . Jen wouldn't have given that up for anything.

"Sylvie said you were at her teacher's house?"

Jen smiled. "Yeah. An old teacher of hers. That's right. I fell asleep on the sofa there."

"Oh. Old teacher? That's not the way I heard it." Pacey arched his eyebrow significantly. "The way I heard it, you fell asleep on some young art teacher's sofa."

Busted. Jen felt her cheeks growing pink.

"If you fell asleep at all," Pacey added.

"Pacey, I did fall asleep," Jen protested immediately. "That's all I did, okay? I'm not the one with a reputation for falling for teachers."

That shut Pacey up for a moment. He scowled.

"And by the way, how did you manage to get so much information from Sylvie? Last time I checked in on you guys, you were down on one knee apologizing, and she was absolutely refusing to forgive you. At least it looked that way to me."

The scowl melted into a smile that tugged at the corners of Pacey's mouth. "Well, let's just say that eventually my many charms won her over."

Jen felt a smile tugging at her lips, too. Pacey and Sylvie. Well, well, well. Jen remembered the hurt in Sylvie's voice when she'd talked about how some people probably thought she wasn't built to be an athlete. From the smile on Pacey's face, it seemed that some people had decided that they liked her just fine the way she was. Jen felt a wave of affection for Pacey.

"So where is Sylvie, anyway? Did she get on the bus already? Ste— Mr. Yarrow sent along her dry clothes with me."

"You'll have to give them to her dad to send to her." Pacey's smile slipped off his face. "She just left by car service to go straight to the airport. Dr. McCann's going to ship her stuff from Capeside."

"Oh. Gee, that's too bad," Jen said, with genuine sympathy. She would have liked to say good-bye to Sylvie herself. After their long hike to get help together, she counted Sylvie as her friend.

Pacey nodded. "Yeah . . . it's too bad." He looked down the road that led away from the school. "Too bad," he said wistfully, "but, hey, it was fun while it lasted. Really fun. And you know what they say: better to have had fun and lost than never to have had fun at all."

Jen looked down the road too, equally wistful. In

her mind, she saw Steve's blue VW fading from view. She didn't bother to remind Pacey that he'd gotten a word wrong. Love, fun . . . whatever it was, she understood what he was saying. "You know what, Pacey? I know exactly what you mean," she said.

It was a perfect day for the time of year. Brilliant blue sky with only a few wispy clouds, the bracing freshness of the salt air, the day crisp but not bitter cold, a few gulls trailing the modest but sturdy ferryboat. Behind them, the small harbor receded, the dozen or so working boats still in the water getting smaller. In front of them, the bay opened out into the ocean—glittering slate-green water dressed with foamy whitecaps from the still rough tides.

Joey leaned against the starboard railing of *The Portuguese Princessa* and took a deep breath of clean sea air. Her classmates flocked to the deck, high spirits ruling in the wake of their adventure. "Hey there, Capesiders!" she heard Marla Adams greeting some of her friends. "Did you hear school's canceled again today?"

Even Abby was taking an intermission from her seasickness, despite the rolling of the boat in the choppy sea. "Joey!" Abby came toward her with a thoroughly put-on 200-watt smile. "We're so glad you're back with the rest of us." She dropped her voice conspiratorially. "How was your night in the love shack with Dawson Leery?"

Not too far away, Dawson was greeting Pacey

with a hearty clap on the back. Joey felt a 200-watt smile of her own stretching across her face. Hers, however, was genuine. Not that she intended to share that with Abby. "Oh, right. I forgot that's what the locals call the place where we spent the night," she said, making herself the picture of sweet innocence. Abby walked away without any information.

But as Joey saw Jen approaching Dawson, she felt the megawatt smile freeze on her face. Jen sashayed across the deck of the *Princessa* and made a beeline right for him.

"Dawson!" she greeted him, energetically enough for Joey and everyone else nearby to hear.

Dawson turned in the direction of her voice. He spotted Jen and grinned.

Jen threw her arms around him in a big hug. Joey felt herself tense up that much more. "Dawson," she heard Jen say, all sugary relief, "I'm so glad you're all right. Wow, I was so worried about you." Jen's arms stayed around Dawson's shoulders. Dawson's hands circled the small of Jen's back.

Just like they've done before, Joey thought. An image forced itself into her mind, an image of Jen and Dawson kissing tenderly, passionately, just the way she and Dawson had last night. Jen knew exactly how Dawson kissed, knew how it felt to be wrapped in his embrace. Joey didn't have an exclusive on that.

The confusion and doubt she'd been feeling the day before came flooding back like aftershocks. She took a step back, intending to flee down to the lower deck of the boat.

But before she could get any farther, Jen was releasing Dawson from her hug and turning toward Joey. She closed the gap between them in two big steps. "Oh, my God, it's so great to see you guys safe," she said.

And before she knew what was happening, Joey was the one caught in Jen's enthusiastic hug. She gave Jen a hug back. What else was she supposed to do? "Hey, Jen," she greeted her. Jen had that particular way of being nice to her just when she was starting to feel sorry for herself. How did Jen always manage to do it? Joey wondered.

"Hey, Joey." Jen gave her a bright but concerned smile. "How are you doing? Are you okay?"

Joey shrugged nonchalantly. "Sure," she said, evenly. "I'm really fine."

"I would have been so terrified out there all night."

Joey sneaked a hand into her front jeans pocket and felt the smooth, hard knob of sea glass. She glanced over at Dawson. He looked right at her, and they shared a private smile with their eyes only. Joey felt her pulse speed up. She looked back at Jen. "Actually, it was . . . kind of fun," she said.

Who knew what would happen in the future? But Joey knew what had happened already, felt the memory of Dawson's kisses, still fresh on her lips.

"Kind of fun?" Jen said. "Well . . . that's kind of good, isn't it?" She gave a tentative laugh.

"Yeah," Joey said, feeling a surge of warmth toward Jen. "It is kind of good. And how about you, Jen? How was it camping out in the school with everyone?"

"Everyone?" Jen said. Was Joey imagining the funny, faraway look on Jen's face? "It was . . . kind of fun," Jen said. The look melted into a smile.

"Well . . . that's kind of good, isn't it?" Joey asked.

Jen nodded. She inhaled deeply. "It looks like it's going to be a beautiful day," she said.

Joey looked out at the open sea and the brilliant sky. The sun shone brightly. She could feel it on her face. "Yeah," she said, nodding. Whatever else was in store in the future, that much looked pretty certain. "A really beautiful day."

"Okay, Dawson, so was it Lina Wertmüller out there last night?" Pacey asked, conspiratorially. "*Swept Away . . . by an Unusual Destiny in the Blue Sea of August.* Sexy European film material?"

Dawson looked his best friend straight in the eye. "*Swept Away?* Pacey, they spoke Italian in that movie. *Buon giorno* is about the extent of my knowledge of that language. And if memory serves me, Giancarlo Giannini played a working-class scrub, part of the crew on some rich guy's boat. And Mariangela Melato—she was the rich guy's spoiled rich wife. What could that possibly have to do with me and Joey?"

Pacey arched an eyebrow. "Okay, Dawson, so then it wasn't *Swept Away.*"

Dawson laughed. "Anyway, what happened to Archie and Betty—or is Joey Veronica?"

The *Princessa* cut through the water and headed out to sea.

Pacey sighed. "Dawson, Dawson. Forget Archie. We've got the foreign thing going here now. A boat, the blue sea, a storm, two people . . . They start out arguing about every little thing. Then they get shipwrecked and fall madly in love. Get down in the sand and—"

"I know, Pacey," Dawson interrupted him. "I've seen the film."

"Right, and I'm sure you watched those down-in-the-sand parts with particular attention," Pacey said with a wry laugh. " 'Fess up, Leery. You can't be as innocent as you pretend to be."

"Me?" Dawson played defense by taking the offense. "What about you? I'm sure you watched those parts with the remote in your hand so you could rewind and play them over and over. And we won't even talk about the other hand."

Pacey shook his head. "Crude, Dawson," he said with false sternness. "And you used to be such a fine, upstanding young man. So . . . ?"

"So how about you, Pacey?" Dawson turned the tables on him. "Did you find your mermaid?"

Pacey laughed. "Oh, I get it. Answer a question with a question. Well, I'll be the bigger man and give you an answer. Did I find my mermaid?" Dawson wasn't sure if he was imagining the funny, faraway look on Pacey's face. "There are no mermaids in real life, Dawson. That's movie stuff." Then the look melted into a smile. "But sometimes reality can be pretty nice," Pacey said.

Dawson glanced over at Joey, who was talking to

Jen at the starboard railing of the boat. Joey looked so pretty, the sea breeze blowing through her long, dark hair, her cheeks pink from the crisp sea air. And Jen, with the sunshine in her blond hair, looked awfully pretty, too. They both did.

Dawson felt a 200-watt smile stretch across his face. "Yeah, I agree with you for once, Pacey," he said. "Sometimes reality can be pretty nice."

About the Creator/Executive Producer

Born in New Bern, North Carolina, Kevin Williamson studied theater and film at East Carolina University before moving to New York to pursue an acting career. He relocated to Los Angeles and took a job as an assistant to a music video director. Eventually deciding to explore his gift for storytelling, Williamson took an extension course in screenwriting at UCLA (University of California, Los Angeles).

Kevin Williamson has experienced incredible success in the film medium. His first feature film was *Scream,* directed by Wes Craven and starring Drew Barrymore, Courteney Cox and Neve Campbell. He has also written other feature films including the psychological thriller *I Know What You Did Last Summer,* based on the Lois Duncan novel, and directed by Jim Gillespie. His first foray into television, *Dawson's Creek*™, has already received high praise from television critics for its honest portrayal of teen life.

About the Author

Jennifer Baker is the author of over thirty novels for young readers and a creator of Web-based entertainment and dramas. She lives in New York City with her husband and son.